PIG TAILS

Traditional tales, fables and legends from around the world about or featuring our porcine friends …

Compiled, Adapted & Edited by Clive Gilson

Tales from the World's Firesides

Pig Tails, edited by Clive Gilson, Solitude, Bath, UK

www.clivegilson.com

First published in 2025

Printed by IngramSpark

ISBN: 978-1-915081-53-7

CONTENTS

Preface

For more than two decades, I have been engaged in the collection and narration of stories, and in recent years I have had the additional satisfaction of publishing some of my own fiction. My creative work has tended to focus on short stories that inhabit the borderlands of magical realism and speculative science fiction, narratives in which the uncanny appears natural and the impossible attains an inner logic.

Folk and fairy tales have consistently remained at the centre of this practice. Over the years, I have assembled a large archive of such narratives from diverse regions of the world, with the longstanding ambition of creating a kind of library, a curated collection that brings together these remarkable stories of people, places, and traditions across cultures.

One of the central motivations for this project is the preservation of tales that might otherwise fall into obscurity. Many of the narratives I engage with derive from the work of early collectors, writing from the late eighteenth century through the nineteenth and early twentieth centuries. Understandably, these collections often reflect the cultural assumptions of their period, especially in relation to issues of race, gender, and colonial perspective. My approach is to adapt such stories with care, aiming to render them accessible to contemporary readers while maintaining fidelity to the imaginative and cultural spirit of the originals.

Equally important is a commitment to treating these traditions with respect. Early collectors frequently framed their material through lenses shaped by colonial attitudes and external judgments of the communities they documented. My objective is not to reproduce such distortions, but rather to preserve and share the narratives in a way that honours their origins. To this end, I have sought to provide full attribution for each tale, including the name of the original collector or author, the textual source, and, wherever possible, the cultural or Indigenous provenance of the story.

This particular volume, *Pig Tails*, is a collection of folk and fairy tales from around the world in which pigs take centre stage. Although pigs may not always inspire the same admiration as more "majestic" animals, there are many compelling reasons to bring these pig-centred stories together.

Pigs occupy a curious and enduring place in the folklore of countless cultures. They have been symbols of prosperity and fertility, embodiments of greed and folly, offerings in ritual and feast, and, in some traditions, guardians of sacred knowledge. Whether portrayed as humble farmyard companions or as monstrous boars of myth, their presence in story carries meanings that are both familiar and deeply symbolic.

In these tales, pigs are not always noble or heroic. More often they are comic, noisy, stubborn, or sly. Yet at times they appear as magical creatures, enchanted princes, or divine beasts whose power rivals that of gods and heroes. This mixture of the ordinary and the extraordinary makes pig stories especially rich. They remind us that even the lowliest of animals may be vessels of wonder.

As in all folklore, shadows accompany the light. There are darker tales here, stories of monstrous boars hunted by kings, of gluttony punished, of vanity unmasked. Yet even these speak to the deep, complicated relationships humans have always had with pigs: as food and sacrifice, as symbols of excess, as figures of laughter, and sometimes, as unlikely teachers of wisdom.

Many of these stories carry moral lessons. Through pigs and boars we are reminded of the dangers of pride, the value of loyalty, the perils of greed, and the strange places where kindness may be found. Like all fairy tales, they lead us into enchanted worlds where animals speak, curses bind, and the line between the comic and the sacred grows thin.

And perhaps most importantly, these tales are fragments of the great oral tradition that threads through every culture. In retelling them, we keep alive not only the stories themselves, but also the voices, values, and imaginations of the people who first gave them shape.

Storytelling is one of the most profoundly human practices. From the earliest days, when people gathered around fires in caves and sought to understand the experience of life, stories have carried our reflections on magic, cleverness, danger, and love. In examining traditions from the Celts, Indonesia, Africa, and the Far East, indeed, from cultures across the globe, it becomes strikingly clear how deeply interconnected we are. The details and costumes of our tales differ, but beneath them the same structural patterns and human concerns persist.

The pig tales collected here, like all folk narratives, encompass joy and sorrow, light and shadow. Some are exuberant and fantastical, while others are quiet and tender, but all reflect essential aspects of human experience. In gathering and retelling these stories, I have been continually reminded of their enduring resonance, and it is my hope that readers may discover within them a sense of wonder and meaning as well.

With warmth and wonder,

Clive

Bath 2025

The Lonely Little Pig

An American Tale

This tale is adapted from a story told by Clara Dillingham Pierson in her book Among the Farmyard People, published by E. P. Dutton And Co., New York, in 1899.

Clara Dillingham Pierson was an American author and folklorist best known for her charming early 20th-century children's books that blend gentle moral lessons with the natural world. While not a folklorist in the academic sense, she contributed to the preservation of oral storytelling traditions by crafting original animal tales in a folkloric style.

One day the Brown Hog called to her twelve young Pigs and their ten older brothers and sisters, "Look! Look! What is in that cage?"

The twenty-two stubby snouts that were thrust through the opening of the rail-fence were quivering with eagerness and impatience. Their owners wished to know all that was happening, and the old mother's eyes were not so sharp as they had once been, so if the Pigs wanted to know the news, they must stop their rooting to find it out. Bits of the soft

1

brown earth clung to their snouts and trembled as they breathed.

"It looks like a Pig," they said, "only it is white."

"It is a Pig then," grunted their mother, as she lay in the shade of an oak tree. "There are white Pigs, although I never fancied the colour. It looks too cold and clean. Brown is more to my taste, brown or black. Your poor father was brown and black, and a finer looking Hog I never saw. Ugh! Ugh!" And she buried her eyes in the loose earth.

The Pigs looked at her and then at each other. They did not often speak of their father. Indeed the younger ones did not remember him at all. One of the Cows said he had such a bad temper that the farmer sent him away, and it is certain that none of them had seen him since the day he was driven down the lane.

While they were thinking of this and feeling rather sad, the wagon turned into their lane and they could plainly see the Pig inside. She was white and quite beautiful in her piggish way. Her ears stood up stiffly, her snout was as stubby as though it had been broken off, her eyes were very small, and her tail had the right curl. When she squealed they could see her sharp teeth, and when she put her feet up on the wooden bars of her rough cage, they noticed the fine hoofs on the two big toes of each foot and the two little toes high on the back of her legs, each with its tiny hoof. She was riding in great style, and it is no wonder that the twenty-two Brown Pigs with black spots and black feet opened their eyes very wide.

They did not know that the farmer brought her in this way because he was in a hurry, and Pigs will not make haste when

2

farmers want them to. The Hogs are a queer family, and the Off Ox spoke truly when he said that the only way to make one hurry ahead is to tie a rope to his leg and pull back, they are so sure to be contrary.

"She's coming here!" the Brown Pigs cried. "Oh, Mother, she's coming here! We're going to see the men take her out of her cage."

The old Hog grunted and staggered to her feet to go with them, but she was fat and slow, so that by the time she was fairly standing, they were far down the field and running helter-skelter by the side of the fence. As she stared dully after them she could see the twenty-two curly tails bobbing along, and she heard the soft patter of eighty-eight sharp little double hoofs on the earth.

"Ugh!" she grunted. "Ugh! Ugh! I am too late to go. Never mind! They will tell me all about it, and I can take a nap. I haven't slept half the time today, and I need rest."

Just as the Mother Hog lay down again, the men lifted the White Pig from the wagon, cage and all, so she began to squeal, and she squealed and squealed and squealed and squealed until she was set free in the field with the Brown Pigs. Nobody had touched her and nobody had hurt her, but it was all so strange and new that she thought it would make her feel better to squeal.

When she was out of her cage and in the field, she planted her hoofs firmly in the ground, looked squarely at the Brown Pigs, and grunted a pleasant, good-natured grunt. The Brown Pigs planted their hoofs in the ground and grunted and stared. They didn't ask her to go rooting with them, and not one of the ten big Pigs or the twelve little Pigs said, "We are glad to see you."

There is no telling how long they would have stood there if the Horses had not turned the wagon just then. The minute the wheels began to grate on the side of the box, every Brown Pig whirled around and ran off.

The poor little White Pig did not know what to make of it. She knew that she had not done anything wrong. She wondered if they didn't mean to speak to her.

At first she thought she would run after them and ask to root with them, but then she remembered something her mother had told her when she was so young that she was pink. It was this, "When you don't know what to do, go to sleep." So she lay down and took a nap.

The Brown Pigs did not awaken their mother, and when they stopped in the fence-corner one of them said to their big sister, "What made you run?"

"Oh, nothing," she said.

"And why did you run?" the little Pigs asked their big brother.

"Because," he answered.

After a while somebody said, "Let's go back to where the White Pig is."

"Oh, no," said somebody else, "don't let's! She can come over here if she wants to, and it isn't nearly so nice there."

You see, they were very rude Pigs and not at all well brought up. Their mother should have taught them to think of others and be kind, which is really all there is to politeness. But then, she had very little time left from sleeping, and it took her all of that for eating, so her children had no manners at all.

At last the White Pig opened her round eyes and saw all the Brown Pigs at the farther end of the field. "Ugh!" said she to herself, "Ugh! I must decide what to do before they see that I am awake."

She lay there and tried to think what her mother, who came from a very fine family, had told her before she left. "If you have nobody to play with," her mother had said, "don't stop to think about it, and don't act as though you cared. Have a good time by yourself and you will soon have company. If you cannot enjoy yourself, you must not expect others to enjoy you."

"That is what I will do," exclaimed the White Pig. "My mother always gives her children good advice when they go out into the world, and she is right when she says that Pigs of fine family should have fine manners. I will never forget that I am a Yorkshire. I'm glad I didn't say anything mean."

So the White Pig rooted in the sunshine and wallowed in the warm brown earth that she had stirred up with her pink snout. Once in a while she would run to the fence to watch somebody in the lane, and before she knew it she was grunting contentedly to herself. "Really," she said, "I am almost having a good time. I will keep on making believe that I would rather do this than anything else."

The big sister of the Brown Pigs looked over to the White Pig and said, "She's having lots of fun all by herself, it seems to me."

Big brother raised his head. "Let's call her over here," he answered.

"Oh, do!" cried the twelve little Pigs, wriggling their tails. "She looks so full of fun."

"Call her yourself," said the big sister to the big brother.

"Ugh!" called he. "Ugh! Ugh! Don't you want to come over with us, White Pig?"

You can imagine how the White Pig felt when she heard this, and how her small eyes twinkled and the corners of her mouth turned up more than ever. She was just about to scamper over and root with them, when she remembered something else that her mother had told her. "Never run after other Pigs. Let them run after you. Then they will think more of you."

She called back, "I'm having too good a time here to leave my rooting-ground. Won't you come over here?"

"Come on," cried all the little Pigs to each other. "Beat you there!"

They ate and talked and slept together all afternoon, and when the Brown Hog called her children home, they and the White Pig were the best of friends. "Just think," they said to their mother, "the White Pig let us visit her, and she is just as nice as she can be."

The White Pig in her corner of the pen heard this and smiled to herself. "My mother was right," she said. "'Have a good time alone, and everybody will want to come.'"

The Hunting of the Calydonian Boar

A Greek Tale

This tale is adapted from a story told by Elsie Finnimore Buckley in her book Children of the Dawn, published by Frederick A. Stokes Co., New York, in 1908

Elsie Finnimore Buckley was a British folklorist, translator, and writer active in the late 19th and early 20th centuries, best known for her work in making classical and folkloric tales accessible to younger readers. Her most notable contribution is "Children of the Dawn: Old Tales of Greece", published in 1908, which retells Greek myths with poetic grace and narrative clarity.

In the ancient city of Calydon, there was great celebration. Queen Althaea had given birth to her first son, Meleager, a future king, if the Fates allowed. Seven days after his birth, the queen lay resting by the fire, her newborn asleep in her arms. Outside, winter cloaked the land, and shadows danced along the walls as the flames flickered.

As she gazed into the fire, Althaea began to dream, not in sleep, but in the half-light of new motherhood. In the shadows, she saw visions: battles and hunts, warriors charging with spears, dogs baying in the chase, and a wild boar crashing through the undergrowth. And in every vision, a single man stood out, tall, proud, and brave. She whispered to her child, hoping he would one day become that hero.

Just as she was drifting into sleep, the warmth of the room suddenly chilled. The wall before her faded into mist, and three towering, otherworldly women stepped silently into her chamber. These were the Fates, Clotho, Lachesis, and Atropos.

Clotho held a thread of life and said, "I give your son a bright, strong life-thread."

Lachesis, with a spindle, said, "I will weave his life through dark places, where his light will shine brightest."

Atropos, silent, walked to the fire and picked up a fallen log. She thrust it deep into the flames until it was burning fiercely. Then, turning to Althaea, she said coldly, "When this brand is completely burned, I will cut his thread. His life ends when the branch is turned to ash."

Althaea screamed, sprang from her bed, and snatched the brand from the fire, stamping it out beneath her gown, burning herself badly. Then, despite her wounds, she hid it away where only she could find it. When her maids found her later, unconscious and burned, they thought it a strange accident. But Althaea told no one what had really happened.

She kept the charred brand hidden. Over time, she bore other children, but Meleager remained her favourite, her fateful secret tied to his soul. And he did grow to be the hero she dreamed of. He was fearless in battle, unmatched with the spear, and beloved by all.

9

When Jason called for heroes to join his quest for the Golden Fleece, Meleager answered. He sailed with the Argonauts and returned covered in glory.

After his return, Calydon was blessed with an abundant harvest. King Oeneus held a great celebration and offered thanks to all the gods, except to Artemis, the huntress. Forgotten, Artemis seethed with anger. One night, she descended from the mountains and whispered into the king's sleeping ear, vowing revenge.

Come spring, her vengeance arrived. A monstrous wild boar emerged from the forests of Arachynthus, destroying fields, trampling vineyards, tearing through flocks, and killing anyone who tried to stop it. No trap could hold it. The people were desperate.

So Meleager called for heroes across Greece to join him in a great hunt. Many came, including great Theseus, Jason, Castor and Pollux, and others. Among the throng was someone unexpected. Atalanta, a fierce huntress from Arcadia, raised in the wild, swift-footed and sharp-eyed, joined the men in the hunt. Unknown to any there was the truth that Artemis herself had sent her.

Though many were sceptical of a woman joining the hunt, Meleager welcomed her, and, in doing so, fell in love. Atalanta was unmoved. She had no interest in love, only in the hunt.

The next morning, they set out. In the thick of the forest, they found the boar's lair. It burst forth, huge and terrifying. It killed dogs and men alike, shaking off spears and traps. Just as it was about to escape, Atalanta loosed an arrow that struck deep behind its ear, and the beast faltered. Meleager rushed forward and drove his spear through its shoulder, and the boar collapsed in the blood-soaked earth.

Meleager declared Atalanta the hero of the hunt, gifting her the boar's head as a trophy. But his uncles, Toxeus and Plexippus, Althaea's brothers, were furious that a woman would claim the prize. In a rage, they insulted Atalanta, but Meleager, unable to bear their scorn or threats, killed them both in a fit of fury.

Realising what he had done, Meleager fled into the forest, haunted by guilt.

News soon reached the palace. Althaea rushed to the gates and saw her brothers' bodies carried on litters. Her grief turned to blind rage. She invoked a terrible curse, calling upon the Furies to hunt down the killer, unaware that it was her own son she had condemned.

When she quickly discovered the truth, her heart broke. She was torn between vengeance and despair. Althaea retreated to her room and pulled out the charred brand from its hiding place. Unable to contain her grief, her hands trembled as she thrust the brand into the flames once more. As the brand burned, so too did Meleager's life begin to fade. Alone in the forest, he collapsed, pursued by invisible horrors. Atalanta, who had followed him in secret, reached him just in time to cradle his head in her lap. He smiled at her, grateful, then died without another word.

Back in Calydon, Althaea watched the last of the brand crumble to ash. Her grief for her brothers and for her son consumed her. She fell beside the fire and died, her heart broken.

That night, Meleager's body was returned to the city by torchlight. Calydon mourned their fallen hero, the saviour of their land, undone by fate, pride, and love.

The Boar With The Golden Bristles

A Dutch Tale

This tale is adapted from a story told by William Elliot Griffis in his book Dutch Fairy Tales for Young Folks, published by Dodd, Mead And Co., New York, in 1918.

William Elliot Griffis (1843–1928) was an American educator, author, and folklorist best known for his pioneering work in introducing Japanese and Korean culture to Western audiences. A former Civil War veteran and Congregational minister, Griffis spent time in Japan during the Meiji Restoration as an educational advisor, where he helped modernise the school system. He also wrote about Korean and Dutch traditions, blending scholarship with storytelling to foster cross-cultural understanding.

In the deep caverns beneath the world, two dwarven blacksmiths were arguing over who was the better metalworker. They decided to settle it with a challenge. They would forge something no one had ever seen. One of them, the dwarf-king, threw gold into the furnace and fanned the flames with the help of another dwarf, who worked the bellows furiously. As the fire roared, a giant fairy disguised

13

as a gadfly flew in and bit the poor bellows-dwarf's hand, but he kept working, teeth gritted, and never stopped.

The fire grew hotter than ever. And from its heart, the dwarf-king pulled a living creature, a boar with bristles of gold. It glowed with heat, its eyes sparked like embers, and it could run faster than lightning. They named it Gullin, meaning "Golden," in the dwarf tongue.

*

Come the time of men, long ago, before farms or fields dotted the land, people in the cold northern lands of what we now call The Netherlands lived off the forest. Men hunted and fished, and women foraged and cooked. No one had ever dreamed of growing food from the ground. They thought that berries, nuts, honey, and acorns were all the earth had to offer. The soil was seen as hard and useless, not something to dig into, let alone plant seeds in.

So the fairies, watching from their hidden realms, took pity on these early people. In their eyes, humans were clever but blind, never guessing at the richness sleeping just beneath their feet. The fairies called a great council and agreed to send down a magical animal, one who could break open the ground and show the people what was possible. With this gift, humankind would begin to discover fields and gardens, wheat and barley, hay for animals, and warm, dry barns to shelter them through winter.

The fairies lived in a distant and radiant place beyond the edge of the world, where clouds glittered and sunshine poured like honey. Among them was a powerful being named Fro, lord of summer rains and golden sunlight. He was beloved by the elves of the White Realm and watched over all things that grew.

Now, in fairy custom, when a baby cuts their first tooth, it's tradition for friends and family to bring gifts. So when Fro, still a tiny fairy child, popped his first tooth, his mother Nerthus was overjoyed. She called everyone together to celebrate, and began to wonder what sort of gift would be worthy of her special boy.

One fairy, as strong as a polar bear and as clever as winter wind, offered an extraordinary idea. He would gift Fro a creature born of fire, an animal who could use its tusks to break the soil and reveal the treasures of the earth.

Gullin was given to young Fro as a gift. And when Fro grew up, he rode the golden boar across land and sky, on errands of sunshine and storm.

But Gullin had a second, quieter gift to give. When not carrying his master, he roamed the earth and taught his wild boar children how to dig deep into the ground. With their tusks, long, sharp, and curved like hooks, they tore open the hard crust of the soil. Where they rooted, the earth softened. Where they passed, flowers bloomed.

At first, the humans didn't know what to make of this. But the children were the first to notice. "Come see!" they cried. "The ground is opening up!" Birds followed the boars, hopping into the little trenches to snatch up worms, singing joyfully as if the earth had finally remembered them.

Soon, people noticed that new plants were growing in those boar-made lines, plants they hadn't seen before. Tall green stalks with heads full of tiny seeds. The children tasted them.

They were delicious! They ate the grains raw, roasted them over the fire, pounded them into meal with stones, and stirred them into honey.

This was how bread first came to the northern world. It started with wild grain, baked on hot stones. Later, the people discovered yeast, and the dough began to rise like magic, bubbling with warmth and air. The women became skilled bakers. They built ovens, kneaded dough, and invented dozens of kinds of bread, from sweet cakes to golden waffles. When they placed meat between slices of bread, they called it broodje, or "little bread", the very first sandwiches.

The people saved seeds from one season to the next. In spring, they planted them in the very trenches the boars had made. And over time, a new word was born from two old ones, "boar" and "row", which became furrow, the word we still use today for lines ploughed in the earth.

Now the men, seeing how much the women had accomplished with what the boars had begun, grew both proud and a little embarrassed.

"It's true," they said, scratching their beards. "The fairies are cleverer than we are. The elves are cleverer. Even the kabouters, the little house-spirits, have more sense. And clearly, our wives are smarter than we ever gave them credit for. But we can't let the boars think they're wiser than us!"

So the men set their minds to work. If animals could open the earth, surely men could too. First, they scratched the ground with sticks. Then they reinforced the sticks with iron. They built frames and handles, and eventually, they invented the plough. For a long time, they pulled it themselves, or harnessed their wives beside them. Only later did they tame oxen and horses to do the heavy work.

Over time, the plough grew more complex, first a knife to cut the clods, then a beam, a mouldboard, handles, and even wheels to keep it straight. The golden tusks of the boar had become tools. And farming was born.

*

Fro, meanwhile, had more than just the golden boar. He owned a magnificent horse named Sleipnir, swift enough to run through fire and sea. He had a magic ship that could carry armies or fold into a cloth. With these, Fro could appear and vanish like a breeze, traveling wherever he pleased.

But time passed, and the golden-bristled boars, once wild teachers of the earth, were hunted to extinction. Yet they were never forgotten. Knights painted boar's heads on their shields and wore them on their armour as signs of courage and cleverness. And when the old temples of Fro were abandoned, people still celebrated Yule, the ancient winter feast. Over time, it became the Christmas season.

Even now, in memory of that magical beast who taught humankind how to feed themselves, a roasted boar's head was carried into great feasts, decorated with rosemary, served on silver dishes, and celebrated with songs and carols.

For the golden boar had given more than meat. He gave humans the idea of the furrow, the promise of the seed, and the first path toward farming, and feasting, together.

The Pig King

An Italian Tale

This tale is my own version of a traditional tale taken from various sources in my own collection of traditional folk and fairy tales.

The tale of "The Pig King" (Il re porco) is one of the classic Italian wonder tales that comes from the 16th-century collection Le piacevoli notti ("The Pleasant Nights") by Giovanni Francesco Straparola.

Straparola's book (published in Venice between 1550–1555) is considered the first European collection of literary fairy tales, predating Basile's Pentamerone and even Perrault. It contains early versions of many story types that folklorists now classify in the Aarne–Thompson–Uther (ATU) index. The Pig King is essentially an "animal groom" tale (ATU 441/425 variants), where a cursed or enchanted husband takes the form of a beast until a bride's love or loyalty frees him.

Long ago in Italy, there reigned a queen who had everything she might desire, palaces of marble, orchards heavy with fruit, and a king who loved her dearly. Yet she had no child, and that was her sorrow.

Every day she prayed, "Heaven, send me a son, and I will love him, whatever he may be."

At last, her prayer was granted. But when the child was born, the queen cried out in astonishment, for he was no ordinary babe. He was a piglet, pink and bristled, squealing and kicking in his golden cradle.

The queen wept, but she kept her vow. "Piglet or prince," she said, "he is my son." And so she raised him as heir to the throne.

The years passed. The pig grew tall and sturdy, clever with his words and shrewd with his wits. Though he wore velvet cloaks over his bristles and a crown upon his snout, still the courtiers whispered and mocked behind his back. But the Pig Prince cared little.

One day he said to his mother, "It is time for me to wed."

The queen, though troubled, obeyed. She sought out the daughters of noble families, and eventually she found three sisters, each fairer than the last.

The eldest was given to the Pig Prince. A wedding feast was held, and though the bride trembled to see her husband's snout, she smiled through her veil. But in the bridal chamber, she whispered scornfully, "I am wed to a beast."

The Pig Prince heard her, and in the morning she was gone, vanished without a trace, though no one dared ask how or where.

The second sister was then given to him. She too was beautiful, and she too spoke cruelly of him. And she too vanished after the wedding night.

At last the youngest sister, who was gentle of heart, came before the queen. "I will wed him," she said, "for he is your son, and if he is kind to me, that is enough."

So the Pig Prince took her as his bride. On their wedding night, the girl sat trembling on the bed. The Pig Prince entered, heavy-hoofed and snorting, and he laid aside his crown. Then, in a voice soft and sorrowful, he said, "Do not despise me, wife. For though I wear this skin, it is not truly mine."

The girl, gathering her courage, laid her hand upon his coarse bristles. "I do not despise you," she whispered. "You are my husband."

At her words, the Pig Prince cast off his skin, and there before her stood a handsome young man, fairer than she had ever dreamed.

"By your kindness, the spell is broken," he said. And he told her then the truth. He had been cursed before his birth to wear the shape of a pig until a bride loved him despite it.

The next morning, when the queen came to see her new daughter-in-law, she found her son radiant and whole, no trace of the pig about him. The courtiers bowed low, astonished, and the queen wept for joy.

But the prince kept his old skin locked in a chest of iron, as a warning of what scorn and cruelty may bring. And it is said that sometimes, in the dark of night, a faint squeal echoes from within, reminding all who hear it that true love sees beneath the skin.

And so the Pig King reigned long and wisely, with his gentle queen beside him, and their story is told to this day in Italy, where folk know that even a pig may be a king, and even a king may wear a pig's face until love reveals his truest form.

The Old Woman And Her Pig

An English Tale

This tale is adapted from a story told by Flora Annie Webster Steel in her book English Fairy Tales, published by Macmillan And Co., Limited, London & Toronto, in 1918.

Flora Annie Webster Steel (1847–1929) was a British writer, folklorist, and colonial administrator's wife best known for her vivid writings about India during the British Raj. Living in India, she developed a deep interest in Indian culture, language, and especially traditional storytelling.

An old woman was sweeping her house, and she found a little crooked sixpence. "What," she said, "shall I do with this little sixpence? I will go to market, and buy a little pig."

So she bought a little pig, but as she was coming home, she came to a stile, and the piggy would not go over the stile.

She went a little further, and she met a dog. So she said to him, "Dog! Dog! Bite pig. Piggy won't go over the stile, and I shan't get home till midnight." But the dog wouldn't bite the pig.

She went a little further, and she met a stick. So she said, "Stick! Stick! Beat dog. Dog won't bite pig, and piggy won't get over the stile, and I shan't get home till midnight." But the stick wouldn't.

She went a little further, and she met a fire. So she said, "Fire! Fire! Burn stick. Stick won't beat dog, dog won't bite pig, pig won't get over the stile, and I shan't get home till midnight." But the fire wouldn't.

She went a little further, and she met some water. So she said, "Water! Water! Quench fire. Fire won't burn stick, stick won't beat dog, dog won't bite pig, pig won't get over the stile; and I shan't get home till midnight." But the water wouldn't.

She went a little further, and she met an ox. So she said, "Ox! Ox! Drink water. Water won't quench fire, fire won't burn stick, stick won't beat dog, dog won't bite pig, pig won't get over the stile, and I shan't get home till midnight." But the ox wouldn't.

She went a little further, and she met a butcher. So she said, "Butcher! Butcher! Kill ox. Ox won't drink water, water won't quench fire, fire won't burn stick, stick won't beat dog, dog won't bite pig, pig won't get over the stile, and I shan't get home till midnight." But the butcher wouldn't.

She went a little further, and she met a rope. So she said, "Rope! Rope! Hang butcher. Butcher won't kill ox, ox won't drink water, water won't quench fire, fire won't burn stick, stick won't beat dog, dog won't bite pig, pig won't get over the stile, and I shan't get home till midnight." But the rope wouldn't.

She went a little further, and she met a rat. So she said, "Rat! Rat! Gnaw rope. Rope won't hang butcher, butcher won't kill ox, ox won't drink water, water won't quench fire, fire won't burn stick, stick won't beat dog, dog won't bite pig, pig won't get over the stile, and I shan't get home till midnight." But the rat wouldn't.

She went a little further, and she met a cat. So she said, "Cat! Cat! Kill rat. Rat won't gnaw rope, rope won't hang butcher, butcher won't kill ox, ox won't drink water, water won't quench fire, fire won't burn stick, stick won't beat dog, dog won't bite pig, pig won't get over the stile, and I shan't get home till midnight."

But the cat said to her, "If you will go to yonder cow, and fetch me a saucer of milk, I will kill the rat." So away went the old woman to the cow.

But the cow said to her, "If you will go to yonder haystack, and fetch me a handful of hay, I'll give you the milk." So away went the old woman to the haystack, and she brought the hay to the cow.

As soon as the cow had eaten the hay, she gave the old woman the milk, and away she went with it in a saucer to the cat.

As soon as the cat had lapped up the milk, the cat began to kill the rat, the rat began to gnaw the rope, the rope began to hang the butcher, the butcher began to kill the ox, the ox began to drink the water, the water began to quench the fire, the fire began to burn the stick, the stick began to beat the dog, the dog began to bite the pig, the little pig squealed and jumped over the stile, and so the old woman got home before midnight.

The Story Of The Three Little Pigs

An English Tale

This tale is adapted from a story told by Joseph Jacobs in his book English Fairy Tales, published by David Nutt, London, in 1890.

Frustrated that British children were growing up on foreign fairy tales, Jacobs set out to collect and retell stories from England, Scotland, Ireland, and Wales in clear, simple English, with a strong ear for storytelling. His collections, especially English Fairy Tales (1890) and Celtic Fairy Tales (1892), include now-iconic versions of stories like "Jack and the Beanstalk," and "Goldilocks and the Three Bears." Many of these tales first appeared in print in his books, and his versions often became the definitive forms that are still told today.

There was an old sow with three little pigs, and as she was very poor, she sent them out to seek their fortune. The first that went off met a man with a bundle of straw, and said to him, "Please, man, give me that straw to build my house."

The man sold the pig his straw, and the little pig built a house with it. Presently along came a wolf, who knocked at the door, and said, "Little pig, little pig, let me come in."

25

To which the pig answered, "No, no, by the hair of my chinny chin chin."

The wolf then answered to that, "Then I'll huff, and I'll puff, and I'll blow your house in."

So he huffed, and he puffed, and he blew the straw house in, and ate up the little pig.

The second little pig met a man with a bundle of furze, and said, "Please, man, give me that furze to build a house."

The man gave the pig his bundle of furze, and the pig built his house. Then along came the wolf, and said, "Little pig, little pig, let me come in."

"No, no, by the hair of my chinny chin chin."

"Then I'll puff, and I'll huff, and I'll blow your house in."

So he huffed, and he puffed, and he puffed, and he huffed, and at last he blew the house down, and he ate up the little pig.

The third little pig met a man with a load of bricks, and said, "Please, man, give me those bricks to build a house with."

So the man gave him the bricks, and he built his house with them. Then the wolf came, just as he had come to the other little pigs, and said, "Little pig, little pig, let me come in."

"No, no, by the hair of my chinny chin chin."

"Then I'll huff, and I'll puff, and I'll blow your house in."

Well, he huffed, and he puffed, and he huffed and he puffed, and he puffed and huffed, but he could not get the house down. When he found that he could not blow the house down, even with all his huffing and puffing, he said, "Little pig, I know where there is a nice field of turnips."

"Where?" said the little pig.

"Oh, in Mr. Smith's Home-field, and if you will be ready tomorrow morning I will call for you, and we will go together, and get some for dinner."

"Very well," said the little pig, "I will be ready. What time do you mean to go?"

"Oh, at six o'clock."

Well, the little pig got up at five, and got the turnips before the wolf came (which he did about six). The wolf said, "Little Pig, are you ready?"

The little pig said: "Ready! I have been and come back again, and got a nice potful for dinner."

The wolf felt very angry at this, but thought that he would get his vengeance somehow or other, so he said, "Little pig, I know where there is a nice apple-tree."

"Where?" said the pig.

"Down at Merry-garden," replied the wolf, "and if you do not deceive me I will come for you, at five o'clock tomorrow and get some apples."

Well, the little pig bustled up the next morning at four o'clock, and went off for the apples, hoping to get back before the wolf came, but he had further to go, and had to climb the tree, so that just as he was coming down from it, he saw the wolf coming along, which, as you may suppose, frightened him very much.

When the wolf came up he said, "Little pig, what... are you here before me? Are they nice apples?"

"Yes, very," said the little pig. "I will throw you one down." And he threw it so far, that, while the wolf was gone to pick it up, the little pig jumped down and ran home.

The next day the wolf came again, and said to the little pig, "Little pig, there is a fair at Shanklin this afternoon, will you go?"

"Oh yes," said the pig, "I will go, so what time will you be ready?"

"At three," said the wolf.

So the little pig went off before that time as usual, and got to the fair, and bought a butter-churn, which he was going home with, when he saw the wolf coming. Then he did not know what to do, so he got into the churn to hide, and by so doing turned it round, and it rolled down the hill with the pig in it, which frightened the wolf so much, that he ran home without going to the fair.

Later he went to the little pig's house, and told him how frightened he had been by a great round thing which came down the hill past him.

Then the little pig said, "Hah, I frightened you, then. I had been to the fair and bought a butter-churn, and when I saw you, I got into it, and rolled down the hill."

Then the wolf was very angry indeed, and declared that he would eat up the little pig, and that he would get down the chimney after him.

When the little pig saw what he was about, he hung a pot full of water over a blazing fire, and, just as the wolf was coming down, took off the cover, and in fell the wolf. The little pig put on the cover again in an instant, boiled him up, and ate the wolf for supper, and lived happy ever afterwards.

The Metal Pig

An Italian Tale

This tale is adapted from a story told by Hans Christian Andersen in the book Fairy Tales of Hans Christian Andersen, published by George H. Doran Co., New York, in 1914.

While Andersen is often grouped with collectors like the Brothers Grimm, who recorded existing folk tales, Andersen crafted new stories inspired by folk motifs but deeply personal in tone and theme. Tales like The Little Mermaid, The Ugly Duckling, The Snow Queen, and The Emperor's New Clothes were his own inventions, blending childlike wonder with subtle social criticism and emotional depth.

In the city of Florence, not far from the Piazza del Granduca, runs a little street called Porta Rosa. In this street, just in front of the market-place where vegetables are sold, stands a pig, made of brass and curiously formed. The bright colour has been changed by age to dark green, but clear, fresh water pours from the snout, which shines as if it had been polished, and so indeed it has, for hundreds of poor people and children seize it in their hands as they place their mouths close to the mouth of the animal, to drink. It is quite a picture to see a half-naked boy clasping the well-formed creature by the head, as he presses his rosy lips against its jaws. Everyone who visits Florence can very quickly find the place, for he has only to ask the first beggar he meets for the Metal Pig, and he will be told where it is.

It was late on a winter evening. The mountains were covered with snow, but the moon shone brightly, and moonlight in Italy is like a dull winter's day in the north, indeed it is better, for clear air seems to raise us above the earth, while in the north a cold, grey, leaden sky appears to press us down to earth, even as the cold damp earth shall one day press on us in the grave.

In the garden of the grand duke's palace, under the roof of one of the wings, where a thousand roses bloom in winter, a little ragged boy had been sitting the whole day long, a boy, who might serve as typical of Italy, lovely and smiling, and yet still suffering. He was hungry and thirsty, yet no one gave him anything, and when it became dark, and they were about to close the gardens, the porter turned him out. He stood a long time musing on the bridge which crosses the Arno, and looking at the glittering stars, reflected in the water which flowed between him and the elegant marble bridge Della Trinita. He then walked away towards the Metal Pig, half knelt down, clasped it with his arms, and then put his mouth to the shining snout and drank deep draughts of the fresh water. Close by, lay a few salad-leaves and two chestnuts, which were to serve for his supper. No one was in the street but himself. It belonged only to him, so he boldly seated himself on the pig's back, leaned forward so that his curly head could rest on the head of the animal, and, before he was aware, he fell asleep.

It was midnight. The Metal Pig raised himself gently, and the boy heard him say quite distinctly, "Hold tight, little boy, for I am going to run," and away he started for a most wonderful ride.

First, they arrived at the Piazza del Granduca, and the metal horse which bears the duke's statue, neighed aloud. The painted coats-of-arms on the old council-house shone like transparent pictures, and Michaelangelo's David tossed his sling, for it was as if everything had life. The metallic groups of figures, among which were Perseus and the Rape of the Sabines, looked like living persons, and cries of terror sounded from them all across the noble square. By the Palazzo degli Uffizi, in the arcade, where the nobility assemble for the carnival, the Metal Pig stopped. "Hold fast," said the animal, "hold fast, for I am going up stairs."

The little boy said nothing. He was half pleased and half afraid. They entered a long gallery, where the boy had been before. The walls were resplendent with paintings, and here stood statues and busts, all in a clear light as if it were day. But the grandest appeared when the door of a side room opened. The little boy could remember what beautiful things he had seen there, but tonight everything shone in its brightest colours. Here stood the figure of a beautiful woman, as beautifully sculptured as possible by one of the great masters. Her graceful limbs appeared to move, while dolphins sprang at her feet, and immortality shone from her eyes. The world called her the Venus de' Medici. By her side were statues, in which the spirit of life breathed in stone, figures of men, one of whom whetted his sword, and was named the Grinder. There were wrestling gladiators forming another group, and the sword had been sharpened for them as they strove for the goddess of beauty. The boy was dazzled by so much glitter, for the walls were gleaming with bright colours, and all appeared in living reality.

As they passed from hall to hall, beauty everywhere showed itself, and as the Metal Pig went step by step from one picture to the other, the little boy could see it all plainly. One glory eclipsed another, yet there was one picture that fixed itself on the little boy's memory, more especially because of the happy children it represented, for these the little boy had seen in daylight. Many pass this picture with indifference, and yet it contains a treasure of poetic feeling. It represents Christ descending into Hades. They are not the lost whom the spectator sees, but the heathen of olden times. The Florentine, Angiolo Bronzino, painted this picture, and most beautiful is the expression on the face of the two children, who appear to have full confidence that they shall reach heaven at last. They are embracing each other, and one little one stretches out his hand towards another who stands below him, and points to himself, as if he were saying, "I am going to heaven." The older people stand as if uncertain, yet hopeful, and they bow in humble adoration to the Lord Jesus. On this picture the boy's eyes rested longer than on any other as the Metal Pig stood still before it. A low sigh was heard. Did it come from the picture or from the animal? The boy raised his hands towards the smiling children, and then the Pig ran off with him through the open vestibule.

"Thank you, thank you, you beautiful animal," said the little boy, caressing the Metal Pig as it ran down the steps.

"Thanks to yourself also," replied the Metal Pig. "I have helped you and you have helped me, for it is only when I have an innocent child on my back that I receive the power to run. Yes, as you see, I can even venture under the rays of the lamp, in front of the picture of the Madonna, but I may not enter the church, even while you are upon my back. I may only look in through the open door. Do not get down yet, for if you do, then I shall be lifeless, as you have seen me in the Porta Rosa."

"I will stay with you, my dear creature," said the little boy.

So then they went on at a rapid pace through the streets of Florence, till they came to the square before the church of Santa Croce. The folding-doors flew open, and light streamed from the altar through the church into the deserted square. A wonderful blaze of light streamed from one of the monuments in the left-side aisle, and a thousand moving stars seemed to form a glory round it. Even the coat-of-arms on the tomb-stone shone, and a red ladder on a blue field gleamed like fire. It was the grave of Galileo. The monument is unadorned, but the red ladder is an emblem of art, signifying that the way to glory leads up a shining ladder, on which the prophets of mind rise to heaven, like Elias of old.

In the right aisle of the church every statue on the richly carved sarcophagi seemed endowed with life. Here stood Michaelangelo, and there Dante, with the laurel wreath round his brow. Alfieri and Machiavelli rest side by side, the pride of Italy. The church itself is very beautiful, even more beautiful than the marble cathedral at Florence, though not so large. It seemed as if the carved vestments stirred, and as if the marble figures they covered raised their heads higher, to gaze upon the brightly coloured glowing altar where the white-robed boys swung the golden censers, amid music and song, while the strong fragrance of incense filled the church, and streamed forth into the square. The boy stretched out his hands towards the light, and at the same moment the Metal Pig started again so rapidly that he was obliged to cling tightly to him. The wind whistled in his ears, he heard the church door creak on its hinges as it closed, and it seemed to him as if he had lost his senses. Then a cold shudder passed over him, and he awoke.

It was morning. The Metal Pig stood in its old place on the Porta Rosa, and the boy found he had slipped nearly off its back. Fear and trembling came upon him as he thought of his mother, for she had sent him out the day before to get some money. He had not done so, and now he was hungry and thirsty. Once more he clasped the neck of his metal horse, kissed its nose, and nodded farewell to it. Then he wandered away into one of the narrowest streets, where there was scarcely room for a loaded donkey to pass.

A great iron-bound door stood ajar, he passed through, and climbed up a brick staircase, with dirty walls and a rope for a balustrade, till he came to an open gallery hung with rags. From here a flight of steps led down to a court, where from a well water was drawn up by iron rollers to the different stories of the house, and where the water-buckets hung side by side. Sometimes the roller and the bucket danced in the air, splashing the water all over the court.

Another broken-down staircase led from the gallery, and two Russian sailors running down it almost upset the poor boy. They were coming from their nightly carousal. A woman, not very young, with an unpleasant face and a quantity of black hair, followed them. "What have you brought home?" she asked, when she saw the boy.

"Don't be angry," he pleaded; "I received nothing, I have nothing at all," and he seized his mother's dress and would have kissed it. Then they went into a little room. I need not describe it, but only say that there stood in it an earthen pot with handles, made for holding fire, which in Italy is called a marito. This pot she took in her lap, warmed her fingers, and pushed the boy with her elbow.

"Certainly you must have some money," she said. The boy began to cry, and then she struck him with her foot till he cried out louder. "Will you be quiet? or I'll break your screaming head," and she swung the fire-pot about which she held in her hand, while the boy crouched to the earth and screamed.

Then a neighbour came in, and she had also a marito under her arm. "Felicita," she said, "what are you doing to the child?"

"The child is mine," she answered; "I can murder him if I like, and you too, Giannina."

And then she swung the fire-pot about even more. The other woman lifted up hers to defend herself, and the two pots clashed together so violently that they were dashed to pieces, and fire and ashes flew about the room. The boy rushed out at the sight, sped across the courtyard, and fled from the house.

The poor child ran till he was quite out of breath, until, at last, he stopped at the church, the doors of which were opened to him the night before, and went in. Here everything was bright, and the boy knelt down by the first tomb on his right, the grave of Michaelangelo, and sobbed as if his heart would break. People came and went, mass was performed, but no one noticed the boy, except for an elderly citizen, who stood still and looked at him for a moment, and then went away like the rest. Hunger and thirst overpowered the child, and he became quite faint and ill. At last he crept into a corner behind the marble monuments, and went to sleep. Towards evening he was awakened by a pull at his sleeve. He started up, and the same old citizen stood before him.

"Are you ill? where do you live? have you been here all day?" were some of the questions asked by the old man. After hearing his answers, the old man took him home to a small house close by, in a back street. They entered a glovemaker's shop, where a woman sat sewing busily. A little white poodle, so closely shaven that his pink skin could plainly be seen, frisked about the room, and gambolled upon the boy.

"Innocent souls are soon intimate," said the woman, as she caressed both the boy and the dog.

These good people gave the child food and drink, and said he should stay with them all night, and that the next day the old man, who was called Giuseppe, would go and speak to his mother. A little homely bed was prepared for him, but to him who had so often slept on the hard stones it was a royal couch, and he slept sweetly and dreamed of the splendid pictures and of the Metal Pig.

Giuseppe went out the next morning, and the poor child was not glad to see him go, for he knew that the old man was gone to his mother, and that, perhaps, he would have to go back. He wept at the thought, and then he played with the little, lively dog, and kissed it, while the old woman looked kindly at him to encourage him. And what news did Giuseppe bring back? At first the boy could not hear, for he talked a great deal to his wife, and she nodded and stroked the boy's cheek.

Then she said, "He is a good lad, he shall stay with us, he may become a clever glovemaker, like you. Look what delicate fingers he has got. Madonna intended him for a glovemaker."

So the boy stayed with them, and the woman herself taught him to sew, and he ate well, and slept well, and became very merry. But at last he began to tease Bellissima, as the little dog was called. This made the woman angry, and she scolded him and threatened him, which made him very unhappy, and he went and sat in his own room full of sad thoughts. This chamber looked upon the street, in which skins hung to dry, and there were thick iron bars across his window. That night he lay awake, thinking of the Metal Pig, indeed, it was always in his thoughts. Suddenly he fancied he heard feet outside going pit-a-pat. He sprung out of bed and went to the window. Could it be the Metal Pig? But there was nothing to be seen as whatever he had heard had passed already.

Next morning, their neighbour, the artist, passed by, carrying a paint-box and a large roll of canvas. "Help the gentleman to carry his box of colours," said the woman to the boy, and he obeyed instantly, took the box, and followed the painter.

They walked on till they reached the picture gallery, and mounted the same staircase up which he had ridden that night on the Metal Pig. He remembered all the statues and pictures, the beautiful marble Venus, and again he looked at the Madonna with the Saviour and St. John. They stopped before the picture by Bronzino, in which Christ is represented as standing in the lower world, with the children smiling before Him, in the sweet expectation of entering heaven, and the poor boy smiled, too, for here was his heaven.

"You may go home now," said the painter, while the boy stood watching him, till he had set up his easel.

"May I see you paint?" asked the boy; "may I see you put the picture on this white canvas?"

"I am not going to paint yet," replied the artist. Then he brought out a piece of chalk. His hand moved quickly, and his eye measured the great picture, and though nothing appeared but a faint line, the figure of the Saviour was as clearly visible as in the coloured picture.

"Why don't you go?" said the painter.

Then the boy wandered home silently, and seated himself on the table, and learned to sew gloves. But all day long his thoughts were in the picture gallery, and so he pricked his fingers and was awkward. But he did not tease Bellissima. When evening came, and the house door stood open, he slipped out. It was a bright, beautiful, starlight evening, but rather cold. Away he went through the already-deserted streets, and soon came to the Metal Pig. He stooped down and kissed its shining nose, and then seated himself on its back.

"You happy creature," he said, "how I have longed for you! We must take a ride to-night."

But the Metal Pig lay motionless, while the fresh stream gushed forth from its mouth. The little boy still sat astride on its back, when he felt something pulling at his clothes. He looked down, and there was Bellissima, little smooth-shaven Bellissima, barking as if she would have said, "Here I am too. Why are you sitting there?"

A fiery dragon could not have frightened the little boy so much as did the little dog in this place. "Bellissima in the street, and not dressed!" as the old lady called it. "What would be the end of this?"

The dog never went out in winter, unless she was attired in a little lambskin coat which had been made for her. It was fastened round the little dog's neck and body with red ribbons, and was decorated with rosettes and little bells. The dog looked almost like a little kid when she was allowed to go out in winter, and trot after her mistress. And now here she was in the cold, and not dressed. Oh, how would it end? All his fancies were quickly put to flight, yet he kissed the Metal Pig once more, and then took Bellissima in his arms. The poor little thing trembled with cold, and the boy ran homeward as fast as he could.

"What are you running away with there?" asked two of the police whom he met, and at whom the dog barked. "Where have you stolen that pretty dog?" they asked, and they took it away from him.

"Oh, I have not stolen it! Give it to me back again," cried the boy, despairingly.

"If you have not stolen it, you may say at home that they can send to the watch-house for the dog." Then they told him where the watch-house was, and went away with Bellissima.

Here was a dreadful trouble. The boy did not know whether he had better jump into the Arno, or go home and confess everything. They would certainly kill him, he thought.

"Well, I would gladly be killed," he reasoned, "for then I shall die, and go to heaven," and so he went home, almost hoping for death.

The door was locked, and he could not reach the knocker. No one was in the street, so he took up a stone, and with it made a tremendous noise at the door.

"Who is there?" asked somebody from within.

"It is I," said he. "Bellissima is gone. Open the door, and then kill me."

Then indeed there was a great panic. Madame was so very fond of Bellissima. She immediately looked at the wall where the dog's dress usually hung, and there was the little lambskin.

"Bellissima in the watch-house!" she cried. "You bad boy! How did you entice her out? Poor little delicate thing, with those rough policemen, and she'll be frozen with cold."

Giuseppe went off at once, while his wife lamented, and the boy wept. Several of the neighbours came in, and amongst them the painter. He took the boy between his knees, and questioned him, and, in broken sentences, he soon heard the whole story, and also about the Metal Pig, and the wonderful ride to the picture-gallery, which was certainly rather incomprehensible. The painter, however, consoled the little fellow, and tried to soften the lady's anger, but she would not be pacified till her husband returned with Bellissima, who had been with the police.

Then there was great rejoicing, and the painter caressed the boy, and gave him a number of pictures. Oh, what beautiful pictures these were! Figures with funny heads, and, above all, the Metal Pig was there too. Oh, nothing could be more delightful. By means of a few strokes, it was made to appear on the paper; and even the house that stood behind it had been sketched in. Oh, if he could only draw and paint! He who could do this could conjure all the world before him.

The first leisure moment during the next day, the boy got a pencil, and on the back of one of the other drawings he attempted to copy the drawing of the Metal Pig, and he succeeded. Certainly it was rather crooked, rather up and down, one leg thick, and another thin, but still it was like the copy, and he was overjoyed at what he had done. The pencil would not go quite as it should, and that he had found out, but the next day he tried again. A second pig was drawn by the side of the first, and this looked a hundred times better, and the third attempt was so good, that everybody might know what it was meant to represent.

And now the glove making went on slowly. The orders given by the shops in the town were not finished quickly, for the Metal Pig had taught the boy that all objects may be drawn upon paper, and Florence is a picture-book in itself for anyone who chooses to turn over its pages. On the Piazza dell Trinita stands a slender pillar, and upon it is the goddess of Justice, blindfolded, with her scales in her hand. She was soon represented on paper, and it was the glovemaker's boy who placed her there. His collection of pictures increased, but as yet they were only copies of lifeless objects, when one day Bellissima came gambolling before him. "Stand still," cried the boy, "and I will draw you beautifully, to put amongst my collection."

But Bellissima would not stand still, so she must be bound fast in one position. He tied her head and tail, but she barked and jumped, and so pulled and tightened the string, that she was nearly strangled, and just then her mistress walked in.

"You wicked boy! The poor little creature!" was all she could utter.

She pushed the boy from her, thrust him away with her foot, called him a most ungrateful, good-for-nothing, wicked boy, and forbade him to enter the house again. Then she wept, and kissed her little half-strangled Bellissima. At this moment the painter entered the room.

*

In the year 1834 there was an exhibition in the Academy of Arts at Florence. Two pictures, placed side by side, attracted a large number of spectators. The smaller of the two represented a little boy sitting at a table, drawing, and before him was a little white poodle, curiously shaven, but as the animal would not stand still, it had been fastened with a string to its head and tail, to keep it in one position. The truthfulness and life in this picture interested everyone. The painter was said to be a young Florentine, who had been found in the streets, when a child, by an old glovemaker, who had brought him up. The boy had taught himself to draw.

It was also said that a young artist, now famous, had discovered talent in the child just as he was about to be sent away for having tied up madame's favourite little dog to use as a model. The glovemaker's boy had also become a great painter, as the picture proved, but the larger picture by its side was a still greater proof of his talent. It represented a handsome boy, clothed in rags, lying asleep, and leaning against the Metal Pig in the street of the Porta Rosa. All the spectators knew the spot well. The child's arms were round the neck of the Pig, and he was in a deep sleep. The lamp before the picture of the Madonna threw a strong, effective light on the pale, delicate face of the child. It was a beautiful picture. A large gilt frame surrounded it, and on one corner of the frame a laurel wreath had been hung. A black band, twined unseen among the green leaves, and a streamer of crepe, hung down from it, for within the last few days the young artist had died.

The Pig Bride

A Korean Tale

This tale is my own version of a traditional tale taken from various sources in my own collection of traditional folk and fairy tales. The tale originates from Korea, and is most often told in rural communities, and belongs to the wide family of animal bride and bridegroom stories found across the globe. In these tales, a human marries a spouse in animal form who is later revealed to be under an enchantment.

The story reflects themes common in Korean folklore: filial duty, the virtue of humility, and the rewards of compassion. It also ties into Korean shamanic and animist traditions, where animals (including pigs) could embody powerful spirits, blessings, or curses. So, while "The Pig Bride" is uniquely Korean in its details and imagery, it shares kinship with other Eurasian "animal bride/bridegroom" tales like the Italian Pig King (Il re porco), the Norwegian East of the Sun, West of the Moon, and even Beauty and the Beast.

Once upon a time in Korea, there lived a farmer with three sons. The eldest was strong, the second was clever, and the youngest was gentle but he spoke very slowly.

One autumn evening, as the red moon bled its light across the rice fields, a shadow moved on the mountain path. It was no deer, no wandering ox, but a wild sow, great and terrible. Her bristles shone like iron spears, her tusks curved like sickles, and when she drew breath, sparks glowed in her nostrils as though a furnace burned within.

The villagers who glimpsed her fled indoors, bolting their shutters and whispering prayers. But the sow walked straight and unhurried to the farmer's gate, her hooves striking the earth like drums of doom.

When she reached the threshold, she raised her head and spoke, not with the grunts of a beast, but in a voice that rumbled like the shifting of mountains, deep and ancient.

"Give me one of your sons to be my husband," she said, "or ill fortune will fall upon this house, and not one stalk of rice will grow in your fields, not one child will live to manhood."

The farmer's knees shook beneath him. His eldest son, broad of shoulder and proud as a cock, stepped back in disgust.

"Wed such a creature? Never! Better to face ruin than shame."

The second son, clever-eyed and sharp-tongued, scoffed aloud. "Who would yoke himself to a swine? Let her go back to her mud."

The sow's eyes, glowing like burning coals, fixed on the father, who stood speechless with fear. He turned at last to his youngest, a quiet boy, gentle in manner, who had always been mocked for his softness.

"My son," the father whispered, voice cracking with despair, "will you save us?"

The boy's heart hammered in his chest, for the sow's gaze pierced him like fire, yet he did not look away. He saw in her eyes something more than hunger, more than threat. He saw a mystery, a sorrow hidden beneath the monstrous form.

And though fear made his hands tremble, he bowed his head, sating, "If it brings peace to our family, then I will marry her."

The earth seemed to grow still at his words. The wind ceased, the crickets hushed, and the red moon, high above, stared down upon the union of man and beast.

So the wedding was held. The bells rang hollow, and though the feast was laid with rice wine and roasted fowl, no laughter carried warmth. The villagers gathered at the edges of the square, whispering behind their hands. Some spat to ward off evil, while others jeered openly, calling the youngest son a fool, cursed forever to share his bed with a beast. Children pointed and laughed as the bride, the monstrous sow, was led grunting through the streets with garlands around her bristled neck, her tusks gleaming in the torchlight like carved ivory.

The boy walked beside her, head bowed, enduring their scorn in silence. The more the people mocked, the prouder the sow seemed to step, as if she relished the shame laid upon him. And so, when night came, they were shut together in the bridal chamber, a single candle sputtering against the darkness.

At first there was only the sound of her breathing, harsh and ragged, and the shuffle of hooves across the floor. Then, as the silence deepened and the world outside grew still, the sow let out a sigh like a storm passing over the mountains. She shuddered, twisted, and in a moment, the skin split apart and sloughed away, falling to the floor like a heavy cloak of bristle and blood.

Before the boy stood not a beast but a woman, radiant beyond mortal measure. Her hair flowed black and as long as a raven's wing, glimmering with blue fire in the candlelight. Her skin shone as pale as moonlight on water, her eyes deep and dark, carrying both sorrow and fierce strength. She moved with a grace that made the very walls seem to bow before her.

She smiled at him then, and though her smile was gentle, it carried the weight of a thousand secrets. "Do not fear," she said, her voice a low melody that echoed like wind through pines. "By day I must wear the skin of the sow, but by night I am as you see me now. If you treat me kindly, with patience and trust, then one day the curse will be broken. And I will be yours, truly, wholly, and forever."

The boy's breath caught in his throat. He looked at the shed skin, still twitching faintly on the floor, and then back at the woman who shone before him like the moon breaking free from storm-clouds. And though fear still lingered at the edges of his heart, something stronger rose to meet it. He was both in awe of his bride , and deeply in love with her.

The youngest son's heart filled with wonder, and he guarded her secret as though it were his own soul. By day, he led her through the village as she wallowed in the mud and grunted like any beast, and the people jeered, shouting out, "There goes the boy who wedded a sow! There go the pig's children, born with bristles hidden beneath their skin!" Their laughter was as a razor blade, but he did not answer them. He walked with his head high, for he knew what they did not, that when night fell and the doors were shut, the beast was gone, and in her place lay the most radiant woman the world had ever seen.

By night she was his beloved, wise, tender, and beautiful beyond telling. Her words carried the gentle hush of rivers, and her eyes glowed with a love that wrapped around him like fire. Together they built a life, and in time she bore him children, strong of limb, fair of face, and bright of spirit. The villagers, blind in their cruelty, spat at the children as though they were born of a sty, but the young man endured their scorn, holding fast to the truth known only to him and his wife.

Years passed, and love bound them more tightly than any curse. But at last, one evening, as the moon climbed high and the night air trembled with silence, his wife came to him with tears shining in her eyes. She took his hands in hers, hands worn and calloused, hands that had carried her burden without complaint, and she whispered, "Husband, the time has come. You must burn the sow's skin. Only then will I be free forever."

Fear struck him, more sharply than any spear. His heart thudded like a drum. "But what if I lose you?" he pleaded. "What if this is a trick of the curse? What if the fire consumes not the skin, but you?"

She cupped his face in her palms and smiled through her tears. "If you love me, trust me. I have walked through darkness beside you, and you have borne shame for my sake. Now let us walk into the light together."

So with trembling hands he lifted the sow's hide, heavy with the stench of earth and blood, and cast it into the flames. The fire roared to life, as bright as the sun, and the skin writhed and twisted, filling the chamber with a terrible squeal, a sound like all the sorrow of the world being burned away. Smoke rose thick and choking, and for a moment he could see nothing but flame and shadow.

Then the fire died down, and the ashes lay cooling upon the hearth. The skin was gone. And in its place, there stood only his true wife, her beauty unveiled, her form radiant, and no longer bound by bristles and curse. She shone like moonlight after storm-clouds, and when she smiled, he knew she would never again be taken from him.

From that day, she lived openly as a woman, and the villagers who had jeered at the pig-bride now bowed low before her wisdom and her beauty. They whispered that she was touched by heaven itself, and that her children were blessed. The youngest son, once pitied and mocked, became the envy of all, for he had won what no gold, no strength, no cunning could claim. He had won the love of a woman who had been both beast and queen of his heart.

And so they lived, raising their children in peace and joy, their love growing only brighter with the years. And if you wander to that village on a clear night, some say you can still hear her laughter, soft as silver bells, rising with the moon that watched over them both.

The Erymanthian Boar

A Greek Tale

The Fourth Labour of Herakles

This tale is adapted from a story from Mary E. Burt and Zénaïde A. Ragozin's book Herakles, the Hero of Thebes, and Other Heroes of the Myth, published by Charles Scribner's Sons, London & New York, in 1900.

Mary E. Burt and Zénaïde A. Ragozin were 19th-century educators and folklorists who contributed to children's historical and literary education by adapting ancient tales and legends for young readers. Mary E. Burt was known for her emphasis on moral and literary development in children, often using classic texts and folklore as educational tools. Zénaïde A. Ragozin, a Russian-American scholar and historian, specialised in making the myths, epics, and early histories of Eastern and Near Eastern civilisations accessible to Western audiences.

Elis is a beautiful plain lying to the north and west of Arcadia. Here once in five years there was a great festival in honour of Zeus, when all the men and boys ran races, wrestled, boxed and played all sorts of games. Between Arcadia and Elis there is a high mountain-range, called

Erymanthos, and a terrible Boar had its lair in those mountains.

The Boar frequently left its den and came down into the plains and killed cattle, destroyed fields of grain and attacked people. Eurystheus, having heard of this Boar, made up his mind that he wanted the beast alive, and so ordered Herakles to bring it to him.

The hero put on his lion skin once more and started for the mountain. On his way he stopped at a little town where the Centaurs had their home. These strange people were half man and half horse. Their home was just on the edge of a high plain, covered with oak-trees and looking down across a wild valley, through which flowed the Erymanthos River. There were many forests and little streams and dreadful gorges in the valley, where these horsemen used to hunt and fish.

The Centaur Chief, Pholos, received Herakles as a guest and gave him cooked meat to eat, while he ate it raw himself, after the Centaurs' custom. When Herakles had eaten his fill, he said to Pholos, "Your food is indeed good and tasteful. But I should enjoy it still more if I could have a sip of wine, for I am very thirsty."

To which Pholos replied, "My dear guest, we have very fine and fragrant wine in this mountain, and I should like nothing better than to give you some of it. But I am afraid to do so, because it has a strong aroma, and the other Centaurs, if they smelt it, might come to my cave and want some. They are very fierce and lawless, and might do you great harm."

"Don't let that trouble you," said Herakles. "I am not afraid of the Centaurs."

So the wine was placed before him and he drank it. In a little while a great noise was heard outside of the cave, a shouting of many wild voices and a stamping of many horses' feet. What Pholos feared had come to pass.

The Centaurs had smelt the fragrance of the wine and in full armour had made for the cave. Then a terrible fight began. The Centaurs fell upon Herakles with pine-branches, rocks, axes, and fire-brands, and the clouds, their mothers, poured a flood of water on him. But Herakles was too clever for them. He put two to flight, prevented others from entering the cave, and shot the rest down with his arrows.

Pholos was a kind-hearted chief, and hearing one of the Centaurs crying for help outside of his cave, went out to him and tried to pull the arrow from his wound, wondering at the same time that so slight a weapon could cause his death. But the arrow slipped out of his hand and struck his own foot. It only made a scratch, but it could not be healed, for the arrow was one of those which Herakles had dipped in the blood of the Hydra, and poor Pholos breathed his last.

The death of his kind host was a great sorrow to Herakles, for in those times, when there was so little safety in travelling, the bond of kindness and gratitude between host and guest was one of the closest and most sacred, often more so than that between members of the same family. In all their later lives, host and guest could never meet as enemies, and if the chances of war brought them face to face as foes, they were not expected to fight. They exchanged greetings and gifts and drove off in different directions.

Herakles therefore sincerely mourned his friend, performed over him the proper funeral rites, and buried him with all due honours in the side of the mountain. There he left him, sore at heart, but comforted by knowing that he had done all he could to reconcile the shade of Pholos, and that his soul would bear him no grudge in Spirit Land.

Then Herakles pressed onward through the wilds of Arcadia, his lion-skin cloak stiff with frost, his breath rising in white clouds against the biting mountain air. He was hunting the terrible Erymanthian Boar, a beast said to be born of Typhon's breath and the winter storms themselves, a creature of such fury and size that even the bravest hunters of the land dared not face it. It was known to ravage entire villages, to gore oxen and men alike with its shining white tusks, and to vanish into the mists before any spear could find its mark.

Herakles tracked it through dark pine forests and over frozen streams, until he caught sight of the monstrous shape rooting in a thicket choked with thorns. With a great shout, he leapt forward, and the beast, startled, crashed through the undergrowth and fled. Onward and upward it charged, carving a path through the snow-draped wilderness, but Herakles was relentless. Higher and higher the chase went, until the boar, as great as a bull and twice as wild, found itself floundering on the summit of Mount Erymanthos. There, the snow lay thick and treacherous, swallowing hooves and slowing even that mighty beast. It roared in frustration and flung gouts of snow into the air with its tusks, but the ground betrayed it, and it could run no more.

Herakles surged forward through the drifts, uncoiling the great net he had brought. With a roar of his own, he cast it wide. The boar bellowed and thrashed, but Herakles fell upon it like a storm, wrestled it down with bare hands, and bound it tight with unbreakable cords. The boar's hot breath steamed in the cold air, and its eyes flashed like fire, but Herakles slung the creature over his shoulder as though it were no heavier than a lamb, and began his long descent from the mountain, his triumph echoing in the wind.

Back in Mykenæ, King Eurystheus, who had once been bold in word, if not in deed, heard the thunderous sound of Herakles approaching. The earth seemed to tremble with each step. And when a guard ran to tell him, breathless, "He carries the Boar alive on his back!" Eurystheus turned pale. Without a word, he scrambled into a great bronze jar kept in the palace courtyard, where he had begun to hide more and more frequently when Herakles returned from his labours.

But Herakles, with a grin fit for a satyr, walked straight to the jar, lifted the lid, and, without ceremony, dropped the bound and furious Erymanthian Boar inside. The beast landed with a snort and a shriek, its massive tusks clanging against the bronze walls. The jar shook with the force of its fury.

Imagine the terror of Eurystheus, trapped within that narrow space, face to face with the monstrous creature he had ordered captured! It is said that he let out a scream that echoed through the palace halls and he leapt from the jar with such speed that he left his royal dignity behind. After that day, he never again dared face Herakles without trembling, and for many moons, he issued his commands from a safe distance, preferably behind thick walls.

The Ox Who Envied the Pig

A Buddhist Tale

This tale is adapted from a story told by Ellen C. Babbitt in her book Jataka tales, published by The Century Co., New York, in 1912.

Ellen C. Babbitt (1872–1939) was an American writer and folklorist best known for her accessible retellings of Eastern fables, particularly from Buddhist and Jataka traditions. Her most notable works include Jataka Tales (1912) and More Jataka Tales (1922), collections of moral stories originally from ancient India, which she adapted for young Western readers. Collaborating with illustrator Ellsworth Young, Babbitt preserved the ethical and philosophical essence of the tales while presenting them in clear, engaging prose.

Long ago, in a valley where the wind sang low through the grass and the hills rolled like sleeping giants, there lived two oxen brothers on a great and busy farm. The elder was called Big Red, strong, steady, and wise. The younger, bright-eyed and impulsive, was named Little Red. Together, they hauled the farmer's carts, ploughed the rich black soil, and turned the heavy millstones from sun-up to twilight.

Their days were filled with toil and dust, but also with rhythm and purpose. Big Red never complained. "The yoke is heavy," he would say, "but it keeps our path straight."

Little Red, however, often looked longingly toward the farmhouse, where softer creatures lived gentler lives.

Now, it happened that the farmer had an only daughter, a sweet-tempered girl with a laugh like the chime of milk pails, and she was soon to be married. The whole household buzzed with preparations. Beeswax candles were poured, fabrics dyed, and barrels of mead rolled in from the village. But the most notable change came in the pigsty.

The Pig, a round and pampered little creature who spent most of his time snoring in the shade, was suddenly treated like royalty. No longer did he root in slop or chew old peels. Now he was fed corn mash soaked in milk, apples sliced fresh from the tree, sweet barley, and even scraps of honeyed bread. The servants brushed his pen, hung fresh herbs to scent the air, and cooed over how "lovely and fat" he was becoming.

Little Red watched this with growing resentment. One evening, as the sun dipped low and the brothers rested in the barn, Little Red stomped his hoof in frustration.

"Brother," he said, "I've had enough of this. Every day we strain beneath the yoke. We eat nothing but dry straw and bitter grass. Meanwhile, that lazy Pig waddles in velvet mud, eats from silver buckets, and does nothing but grunt!"

Big Red chewed slowly, his large eyes patient beneath his thick brow. "Do not envy him," he said at last. "That pig is not being honoured, he is being prepared. The sweet food he eats is not a reward. It is a path. And it leads straight to the cookpot."

Little Red snorted. "Then let him have his pot. I'd take one day of cream and apples over a hundred of hay and hauling."

But Big Red only sighed. "Better a plain life that endures than a rich one cut short."

Days passed, and the wedding day drew near. The farm buzzed louder than ever. On the morning of the feast, Little Red was awakened not by the crow of the rooster, but by a strange silence. The Pig's pen stood open, and his soft bed of straw was empty.

Then came the smell of roasting meat, herbs sizzling in fat, and the unmistakable sweetness of apple stuffed into something far less lucky.

Little Red watched from the edge of the barnyard as guests arrived in fine linen, laughing, dancing, and praising the feast. He saw servants carrying out great platters. And in the centre of the longest table, his eyes fixed on the shining apple clamped in the pig's mouth.

That night, the oxen stood quietly under the stars. "Do you understand now?" Big Red asked gently.

Little Red lowered his head. "Yes, brother," he said. "His life was rich for a moment... and then gone. Ours may be humble, but we rise with the sun and greet it again the next day."

Big Red nodded. "There is wisdom in plain straw. It may not delight the tongue, but it fills the belly for many seasons."

And so, the two oxen returned to their work with peace in their hearts. The seasons came and went. The wedding guests forgot the feast. The cook stirred new pots. But in the fields, Big Red and Little Red walked steadily, side by side, living long, working true, and never again envying the pig.

The Comic–Heroic Cycle of Pigsy

A Chinese Story Cycle

These tales are my own versions of a traditional tale cycle taken from various sources in my own collection of folk and fairy tales. The comic–heroic tales of Pigsy (Zhu Bajie) come from the great 16th-century Chinese novel Journey to the West (Xī Yóu Jì, 西游记), traditionally attributed to the writer Wu Cheng'en.

Pigsy's character, part human, part pig spirit, is one of the four central pilgrims who accompany the monk Tripitaka (Tang Sanzang) on his quest to India for the Buddhist scriptures. His "cycle" of episodes, his gluttony, laziness, blunders, comic disguises, and yet surprising bravery, aren't a separate folk-tale collection but rather woven throughout the larger novel.

That said, Journey to the West itself drew deeply on Chinese oral folklore, Buddhist parables, and Daoist popular tales that had been circulating for centuries.

I. Pigsy Joins The Pilgrimage

Long ago, when Heaven cast him down for drunken folly, Zhu Bajie, also known as Pigsy, wandered in shame across the earth. He lived in mountains, raided fields, and at last settled in a small village, where he terrorised the farmers until they tricked him into meeting the holy monk Tripitaka.

The monk spoke kindly to him, and for the first time, Pigsy felt the stirrings of hope. He bowed his great head, tusks gleaming, and swore to serve the monk as a disciple, though secretly he muttered, "If there's food on this journey, I'll follow him anywhere."

So Pigsy joined the company alongside Sun Wukong the Monkey King, fierce and clever, Sha Wujing the Sand Monk, grim and patient, and Tripitaka, pure-hearted and as fragile as a reed.

The pilgrims laughed often at Pigsy's laziness and endless hunger, but even from the start, he proved useful. For when brigands came howling out of the hills, it was Pigsy who sent them running with his great nine-toothed rake, roaring as if a thousand hogs had charged the field.

II. Pigsy And The Melon Feast

Once, the pilgrims entered a village starving after weeks on the road. Monkey sent Pigsy to beg food, knowing full well he could not be trusted.

Pigsy waddled through the village lanes, his snout sniffing out every pot. At last, he saw a garden heavy with melons. He swore to himself, "I will only taste one." But one melon became two, two became four, until he rolled on the ground, clutching his belly.

When he returned to his companions, all he carried was a single cracked rind. Monkey seized him by the ear. "Greedy hog! What have you done?"

Pigsy rubbed his stomach and sighed. "I tasted them only to be sure they were safe. It would be unkind to poison the master!"

Tripitaka shook his head in dismay, and Sha Wujing said nothing, though his eyes rolled heavenward.

But as they quarrelled, angry farmers came rushing, crying that a thief had raided their fields. Monkey would have beaten Pigsy then and there, but seeing the furious villagers with sticks and hoes, Pigsy swung his great iron rake to protect the monk. He scattered the farmers, not out of nobility but sheer desperation to save his own hide.

In the end, it was Pigsy's blunder that brought both shame and safety. He had eaten the melons, yes, but in fending off the angry villagers, he unwittingly shielded Tripitaka from harm.

Monkey laughed until his sides hurt. "Brother Pig, only you could turn theft into heroism!"

And Pigsy, licking melon juice from his tusks, grinned and replied, "Every pig has his purpose!"

III. Pigsy And The River Demon

The pilgrims came one day to a river as broad as the sea. Its waves roared, and fishermen whispered of a demon beneath who swallowed whole boats.

Pigsy strutted forward. "This is my time to shine. I am half fish already, I love water!" And before anyone could stop him, he leapt in.

No sooner had Pigsy splashed into the water than the calm surface shattered. The river began to churn and froth as if it boiled from within. From the depths surged a demon, vast and terrible, his body scaled like a dragon, his jaws gaping wide enough to swallow an ox whole. His eyes glowed red beneath the waves, and his voice thundered, "Who dares disturb my river?"

Pigsy thrashed wildly, his ears flapping, his tusks clacking in terror. "Help, brothers! Help me, or I'll be soup!" he squealed, kicking his legs like a child thrown into a pond. The demon coiled around him, claws raking the water, and dragged him beneath the surface.

From the riverbank, Monkey doubled over with laughter, tears rolling down his furry cheeks. "Pig-head! You've leapt straight into the pot!" But when the waters foamed crimson, even he grew serious. With a cry, Monkey leapt high into the air and plunged down, his golden staff blazing like lightning.

The demon turned with a roar, his tail lashing like a whip. Pigsy bobbed to the surface, coughing and squealing, while Monkey's staff crashed against the demon's armoured hide. Sparks flew. Sha Wujing, silent and grim, waded into the torrent with his monk's staff, striking from below. The river shook with their battle, waves slamming against the banks as if a storm had burst from nowhere.

Pigsy, emboldened, gripped his iron rake. "If I'm to be eaten, I'll give him indigestion first!" he bellowed, and with surprising fury, he swung. The rake's nine teeth raked across the demon's snout, tearing scales free. The monster howled, the sound echoing through the mountains.

"Strike him again!" Monkey shouted, springing high and bringing his golden staff down upon the demon's skull. Sha Wujing thrust low, splitting the current. Pigsy, squealing like ten thousand hogs, rammed forward, his rake biting deep into the demon's jaw.

At last, bleeding and beaten, the river demon fled back into the depths, vanishing in a whirlpool that swallowed its own roar. The waters stilled, though they ran red with blood for a long time after.

Pigsy crawled onto the bank, water streaming from his snout and ears. He collapsed on the grass, wheezing, then puffed out his chest. "Well," he said proudly, "that went exactly as I planned. I knew if I jumped in first, he'd show himself. You're welcome."

Monkey burst into fresh laughter, clutching his belly. "Planned? You sank like a stone and squealed like a pig at slaughter!"

But Tripitaka raised his hands in blessing. "Even so, it was Brother Pig's recklessness that lured the demon out. And so Heaven writes straight with crooked lines."

Pigsy grinned through his tusks, secretly pleased, and muttered, "Crooked or straight, I'd rather write with a bowl of rice."

IV. Pigsy And The Hungry Spirit

One evening, after many weary miles on the road, the pilgrims came upon a poor family's hut, its roof sagging, its hearth cold. Inside, a mother and father bowed low, their faces drawn as thin as paper. Their children peered out from behind them, pale and wide-eyed, their bellies hollow with hunger.

Still, the family, though they had little, placed before the travellers all they could spare, which was a pot of watery porridge that gave off more steam than substance, and a few withered greens that looked as though they had already died once in the field.

Tripitaka received the offering with folded hands. "Heaven bless your kindness," he said.

Pigsy's eyes, however, bulged. His ears twitched, his tusks dripped with saliva, and his stomach growled so loudly that the rafters shook. He licked his snout and muttered, "This will hardly feed a sparrow, let alone a warrior of my stature."

Monkey grinned slyly. "Brother Pig, I thought you claimed to eat like a bird. A vulture, perhaps."

Pigsy scowled but said no more. When the bowls were set before them, he leaned close, his nose hovering over the thin porridge, and his heart ached, not from hunger, but from the sight of the children staring, their eyes fixed on the food they had given away.

With a great sigh, Pigsy pushed his portion toward the little ones. "Eat, little piglets," he whispered. "I am full already."

The children blinked in surprise, then devoured the porridge greedily. Pigsy turned away, his stomach roaring like a temple drum.

That night, as they lay upon mats of straw, Pigsy rolled back and forth, clutching his belly, groaning loudly. "Oh, I should never have eaten so much! I am undone, overstuffed, bursting!"

Monkey snorted with laughter. "Ha! Stuffed with what, Brother Pig? Air?"

Tripitaka frowned with pity. "Poor Pigsy, you never learn moderation. Heaven grant your belly peace."

Sha Wujing said nothing, though the corners of his mouth twitched as he turned over to sleep.

Only the children, hidden in their corner, knew the truth. They whispered to one another that the pig-faced spirit had saved them from hunger. And years later, when they were grown, they told the tale often, that a creature mocked as greedy and gluttonous had once gone hungry for their sake.

And some say that in the telling, they always added with a laugh, "But never tell Pigsy's story without his groans! For even his kindness had to squeal."

V. Pigsy And The Mountain of Brides

The pilgrims came to a valley shadowed by black cliffs, where the cries of sorrow carried from every house. The villagers fell at Tripitaka's feet, weeping, and told their tale:

"Every season, the Demon Lord of the Mountain sends his servants. He demands a maiden for his bride, and if we refuse, he devours tenfold in rage. Our daughters are taken one by one, and none return."

Tripitaka clasped his hands in pity. Monkey's tail lashed with fury. Sha Wujing's brow darkened. But before they could speak, Pigsy waddled forward, puffing out his chest, tusks gleaming in the lamplight.

"Do not fear, good people," he boomed. "I, Zhu Bajie, will go as a bride myself!"

The villagers blinked in astonishment. Then, one by one, they burst into helpless laughter. "You? A bride? With a snout like a shovel and ears like banners?"

But Pigsy was undeterred. He snorted proudly. "When I am veiled, no demon will know the difference. And when he tries to lift the veil, then he will meet my rake."

So the women of the village set to work. They dressed him in silks, tied his flapping ears back with crimson ribbons, and powdered his snout until it shone white. They draped a scarlet veil across his face, hiding his tusks, though his belly bulged so large beneath the gown that all shook with laughter again.

Tripitaka sighed. Monkey fell into the dust, howling with mirth. "Oh, Pig-head," he gasped, "if beauty alone could slay demons, you'd already have won!"

But Pigsy only fluttered his lashes and minced his steps, swaying like a maiden. "Watch and learn," he said grandly.

That night, the demon's servants came to claim the "bride" and led Pigsy up the mountain. They brought him into the cavern, as vast as a palace, lit by torches burning blue. There upon a throne of bones sat the Demon Lord, a monstrous figure with horns curling from his brow and eyes like pits of fire.

"Ah, my lovely," he growled, rising to seize his prize.

Pigsy trembled, but remembered his plan. He fluttered his lashes, squealed softly, and stepped forward, swaying like a coy maiden. The demon stretched out his claws, eager to lift the veil...

And in that instant, Pigsy roared like a thunderclap, tore off the veil, and swung down his nine-toothed rake with all his might. The crash shook the cavern, scattering bones in every direction. The Demon Lord howled in fury, the cavern walls quaking with his rage.

At once Monkey burst in, his golden staff blazing, and Sha Wujing surged forward with his monk's staff. The cavern erupted in battle, Monkey darting like lightning, Sha striking like a hammer, and Pigsy bellowing as he swung his rake, each blow shaking the ground. The stolen maidens, huddled in chains, cried out in terror and hope.

The fight raged long, the demon lashing with claws and tail, but at last, with a final combined strike, the three disciples brought him low. His body crashed to the earth, and the cavern rang with silence.

Pigsy straightened his tattered gown, brushed ash from his powdered snout, and puffed out his chest. "Behold," he declared to the wide-eyed maidens, "your rescuer, the Unlikely Bride!"

When they returned the girls to the village, the people lifted Pigsy on their shoulders, half laughing, half cheering. From that day forward, the story spread far and wide of the pig-spirit who dressed as a maiden and slew a demon lord. And though Monkey mocked him without mercy, still the name clung to him, *The Unlikely Bride*, a title that spread even faster than his belly.

VI. Pigsy's Heart

Through all these long years of wandering, Pigsy complained, bumbled, and stumbled. He ate too much, he slept too long, and when there was work to be done, he was usually the first to disappear behind a tree or pretend to be ill. He quarrelled with Monkey, sulked when scolded, and sometimes brought more trouble than he solved.

And yet, when the path grew dark with demons, it was Pigsy who planted his feet and swung his iron rake with a roar. When Tripitaka faltered, it was Pigsy who bent his broad back to carry the master across streams or through the mud, grumbling all the while but never once letting him fall. And when the nights grew cold, and their campfires small, it was Pigsy's booming laughter and endless appetite that gave the company a kind of warmth no blanket could provide.

He was not clever like Monkey, nor pure like Tripitaka, nor steady like Sha Wujing. But he was always there, loyal, fierce when roused, and in his clumsy, muddle-headed way, kind. If a child cried, he would slip them his rice bun. If a villager went hungry, he would grumble and pretend to be selfish, yet later they would find their pantry mysteriously fuller. Pigsy never boasted of these things. He left others to laugh at his pig's snout while he bore it with a shrug and a sigh.

VII. Pigsy's Reward At The Journey's End

After fourteen years upon the road, through deserts, mountains, and demon-haunted lands, the pilgrims at last reached their goal, the Thunder Monastery in the Western Heaven. There, amid halls that shone with golden light, they received the sacred scriptures, treasures of wisdom to bring back to China.

Monkey stood proud, his staff gleaming. Sha Wujing bowed in silence, his face grave. Tripitaka wept with joy, for his quest was fulfilled.

And Pigsy? He leaned upon his great rake, his belly full as he had been feasting on offerings, and muttered, "At last! Perhaps now I can sleep without someone shaking me awake for night-watch."

But Heaven had not forgotten his service. When the scriptures were borne home and the Jade Emperor looked upon the pilgrims, he decreed rewards for each. Tripitaka became a Buddha of purest virtue. Monkey was made a Victorious Buddha, his sins burned away by devotion. Sha Wujing was raised to a golden bodhisattva.

Then all eyes turned to Pigsy.

The courtiers of Heaven whispered, "What can be done with this one? He is greedy, lazy, and forever complaining. Yet, he bore hardships, fought demons, saved the monk, and never forsook his companions."

So the Jade Emperor smiled and spoke, "Zhu Bajie, though your belly is great and your appetites greater, your loyalty has never faltered. You are not fit to be a Buddha, nor yet a bodhisattva, but you shall hold a place in Heaven all the same. From this day forth, you shall be Marshal of the Cleanser of Altars. You will receive offerings, tend the banquets of the gods, and never lack for food again."

At this, Pigsy's ears perked up, and his snout twitched with joy. He fell upon his knees, squealing, "Heaven is merciful! At last I am given a post that suits me

The Sagacious Monkey And The Boar

A Japanese Tale

This tale is adapted from a story told by Yei Theodora Ozaki in the book Japanese Fairy Tales, published by Macmillan And Co., Limited, London & Toronto, in 1912.

Yei Theodora Ozaki (1871–1932) was a pioneering Japanese-British writer and translator best known for bringing traditional Japanese fairy tales and legends to English-speaking audiences. The daughter of a Japanese nobleman and an Englishwoman, Ozaki grew up between cultures and used her unique perspective to bridge East and West. Her most celebrated work, Japanese Fairy Tales (1903), remains a classic, offering elegant, accessible retellings of stories drawn from Japanese folklore, mythology, and oral tradition.

Long, long ago, there lived in the province of Shinshin in Japan, a traveling monkey-man, who earned his living by taking round a monkey and showing off the animal's tricks.

One evening the man came home in a very bad temper and told his wife to send for the butcher the next morning.

The wife was very bewildered and asked her husband, "Why do you wish me to send for the butcher?"

"It's no use taking that monkey round any longer, he's too old and forgets his tricks. I beat him with my stick, but he won't dance properly. I must sell him to the butcher and make what money out of him I can. There is nothing else to be done."

The woman felt very sorry for the poor little animal, and pleaded for her husband to spare the monkey, but her pleading was all in vain, for the man was determined to sell him to the butcher.

Now the monkey was in the next room and overheard every word of the conversation. He soon understood that he was to be killed, and he said to himself, "Barbarous, indeed, is my master! I have served him faithfully for years, and instead of allowing me to end my days comfortably and in peace, he is going to let me be cut up by the butcher, and my poor body is to be roasted and stewed and eaten! Woe is me! What am I to do… Ah, a bright thought has struck me! There is a wild boar living in the forest nearby. I have often heard tell of his wisdom. Perhaps if I go to him and tell him the strait I am in he will give me his counsel. I will go and try."

There was no time to lose. The monkey slipped out of the house and ran as quickly as he could to the forest to find the boar. The boar was at home, and the monkey began his tale of woe at once.

"Good Mr. Boar, I have heard of your excellent wisdom. I am in great trouble, and you alone can help me. I have grown old in the service of my master, and because I cannot dance properly now he intends to sell me to the butcher. What do you advise me to do? I know how clever you are!"

The boar was pleased at the flattery and determined to help the monkey. He thought for a little while and then said, "Does your master have a baby?"

"Oh, yes," said the monkey, "he has one infant son."

"Doesn't it lie by the door in the morning when your mistress begins the work of the day? Well, I will come round early and when I see my opportunity I will seize the child and run off with it."

"What then?" said the monkey.

"Why the mother will be in a tremendous scare, and before your master and mistress know what to do, you must run after me and rescue the child and take it home safely to its parents, and you will see that when the butcher comes they won't have the heart to sell you."

The monkey thanked the boar many times and then went home. He did not sleep much that night, as you may imagine, for thinking of the coming morning. His life depended on whether the boar's plan succeeded or not. He was the first up, waiting anxiously for what was to happen. It seemed to him a very long time before his master's wife began to move about and open the shutters to let in the light of day. Then all happened as the boar had planned. The mother placed her child near the porch as usual while she tidied up the house and got her breakfast ready.

The child was crooning happily in the morning sunlight, dabbing on the mats at the play of light and shadow.

Suddenly there was a noise in the porch and a loud cry from the child. The mother ran out from the kitchen to the spot, only just in time to see the boar disappearing through the gate with her child in its clutch. She flung out her hands with a loud cry of despair and rushed into the inner room where her husband was still sleeping soundly.

He sat up slowly and rubbed his eyes, and crossly demanded what his wife was making all that noise about. By the time that the man was alive to what had happened, and they both got outside the gate, the boar had got well away, but they saw the monkey running after the thief as hard as his legs would carry him.

Both the man and wife were moved to admiration at the plucky conduct of the sagacious monkey, and their gratitude knew no bounds when the faithful monkey brought the child safely back to their arms.

"There!" said the wife. "This is the animal you want to kill? If the monkey hadn't been here we should have lost our child forever."

"You are right, wife," said the man as he carried the child into the house. "You may send the butcher back when he comes, and now give us all a good breakfast and the monkey too."

When the butcher arrived he was sent away with an order for some boar's meat for the evening dinner, and the monkey was petted and lived the rest of his days in peace, nor did his master ever strike him again.

The Man Who Became A Pig

A Korean Tale

This tale is adapted from a story told by Pang Im and Yuk Yi in the book Korean Folk Tales - Imps, Ghosts And Fairies, compiled by James Scarth Gale and published by J. M. Dent & Sons Ltd., London, in 1913.

Pang Im (better known as Im Bang, 1640–1724) and Yuk Yi (often rendered Yi Ryuk/Yi Yuk, traditionally dated 1438–1498) were Joseon-era scholar-literati whose anecdotal "yadam" writings, mixing ghost lore, moral exempla, and everyday satire steeped in Confucian, Buddhist, and Daoist motifs, became key sources for early English presentations of Korean folklore. Their tales (drawn from circulating manuscripts and later reprints) were translated and popularised by missionary-scholar James Scarth Gale in Korean Folk Tales: Imps, Ghosts and Fairies (1913), which helped introduce Korean supernatural and folk narratives to Western readers.

A certain Minister of State, called Kim Yu, living in the County of Seung-pyong, had a relative who resided in a far-distant part of the country, an old man aged nearly one hundred. On a certain day a son of this patriarch came to the office of the Minister and asked to see him. Kim ordered him to be admitted, and inquired as to why he had come. He said, "I have something very important to say, a private matter to lay before your Excellency. There are so many guests with you now that I'll come again in the evening and tell it."

In the evening, when all had departed, he came, and the Minister ordered out his personal retainers and asked the meaning of the call. The man replied, saying, "My father, though very old, was, as you perhaps know, a strong and hearty man. On a certain day he called us children to him and said, 'I wish to have a siesta, so now close the door and all of you go out of the room. Do not let anyone venture in till I call you.'

"We children agreed, of course, and did so. Till late at night there was neither call nor command to open the door, so that we began to be anxious. We at last looked through the chink, and there was our father changed into a huge pig! Terrified by the sight of it we opened the door and looked in, when the animal grunted and growled and made a rush to get out past us. We hurriedly closed the door again and held a consultation.

"Some said, 'Let's keep the pig just as it is, within doors, and care for it.' Some said, 'Let's have a funeral and bury it.' We ignorant country-folk not knowing just what to do under such peculiar circumstances, I have come to ask counsel of your Excellency. Please think over this startling phenomenon and tell us what we ought to do."

Prince Kim, hearing this, gave a great start, thought it over for a long time, and at last said, "No such mysterious thing was ever heard of before, and I really don't know what is best to do under the circumstances, but still, it seems to me that since this metamorphosis has come about, you had better not bury it before death, so give up the funeral idea. Since, too, it is not a human being any longer, I do not think it right to keep it in the house. You say that it wants to make its escape, and as a cave in the woods or hills is its proper abode, I think you had better take it out and let it go free into the trackless depths of some mountainous country, where no foot of man has ever trod."

The son accepted this wise counsel, and did as the Minister advised. He took the man-pig away into the deep mountains and let it go. Then he donned sackcloth, mourned, buried his father's clothes at the funeral, and forever afterwards the family has observed the day of metamorphosis as a day of sacrificial ceremony.

Twrch Trwyth

An English Story

This tale is my own versions of a traditional Arthurian legend taken from various sources in my own collection of folk and fairy tales. The tale of Twrch Trwyth originates from early Welsh mythology, preserved in the medieval prose tales of the Mabinogion. Specifically, it appears in the story "Culhwch and Olwen", which is the oldest surviving Arthurian tale (recorded in Middle Welsh around the 11th century, though drawing on much older oral traditions).

So the origin of the tale is in early Celtic oral myth, written down in medieval Wales (11th–12th century), but its roots are likely pre-Christian, tied to ancient Celtic boar-hunting legends where the boar symbolised both fertility and ferocity.

When Arthur was High King and the island of Britain lay under his protection, there was said to be no beast so fierce, no creature so deadly, as Twrch Trwyth, the monstrous boar.

He was no ordinary animal. Once, they say, he had been a prince of men, proud and cruel, cursed by God to wear the shape of a beast. In that shape his fury only grew. His back was as broad as a hill, his tusks sharper than swords, and his bristles glittered like spears in the sun. Wherever Twrch

Trwyth ran, villages burned, crops withered, and men were trampled into the earth. None dared hunt him, for he was followed by seven other enchanted boars, his sons, each terrible in their own right.

But Arthur was never one to turn from peril. A giant's daughter had set him a quest. To win her hand, he must obtain the comb and shears carried in Twrch Trwyth's mane. Without them, she would not wed. So Arthur gathered his war-band and his hounds, and they swore to hunt the boar across all the lands of Britain and into Ireland itself.

The first time they sighted Twrch Trwyth was on the high, wet slopes of Ireland, where the mist clung to the mountains and the rivers ran red with autumn clay. At first the ground trembled, a low rumble beneath their horses' hooves. Then the beast came into view, breaking through the trees like a thunderbolt.

He was vast beyond imagining. His back rose higher than a warhorse, his bristles stiff as spearheads, glittering with dew and blood. Foam gushed from his slavering mouth, and every breath steamed from his tusked jaws like the smoke of a forge. Wherever he set his hooves, earth split and rocks tumbled, as if the land itself could not bear his weight.

Arthur's hounds leapt forward, baying like war-horns, their cries rolling through the valleys. They flung themselves at the beast's heels, teeth snapping, but Twrch Trwyth kicked them aside like dry leaves. The knights spurred their chargers, lances levelled, their banners streaming. Steel flashed, arrows flew, but the boar's hide turned most blows as though it were iron.

Then he charged.

Men were thrown aside like rag-dolls, split upon his tusks as though they were scythes reaping human grain. Horses screamed as they were gored, knights toppled beneath his fury. Entire villages fled at the sound of his coming, for his bellow carried like a storm-wind, and the thunder of his hooves was like a hundred drums of war.

Arthur himself rode at the forefront, Caledfwlch, the mighty sword later called Excalibur, raised high. He and his war-band encircled the beast upon the slope, spears glittering, shields locked. But Twrch Trwyth did not fear them. With a roar that shook the heavens, he hurled himself against their line. The shield-wall splintered, men screamed, and the boar burst through like a storm through a forest thicket, scattering them in ruin. Blood marked his trail, and still he thundered on, his tusks wet and gleaming.

Yet Arthur did not falter. He rose from the wreckage, his sword red in his fist, and swore aloud so that Heaven and Earth could hear, "By my crown, no beast, no man, no monster shall ever boast of escaping Arthur, King of the Britons! I will hunt you to the world's edge, Twrch Trwyth, until either you fall, or I!"

And at those words, the hunt was bound by fate itself, and all the isles would soon echo with the terror of it.

From Ireland, the hunt drove Twrch Trwyth into the sea. Foam rose in mountains around him as his colossal body struck the waves, and spray glittered like shattered glass beneath the red of the dawn. His seven sons swam close behind, their eyes burning, their tusks slicing the water like blades. Never before had the channel between Ireland and Wales been so churned, the waves roaring as if in terror of the beast that crossed them.

Behind him came Arthur's fleet, sails straining against the wind, oars biting the sea in furious rhythm. Trumpets blared, and the war-cries of Britain echoed over the waves. The knights on the decks gripped their spears and shields, their eyes fixed on the monstrous shapes breasting the foam ahead.

At length, with a sound like thunder rolling through the cliffs, the boars struck land in Dyfed. Water cascaded from their bristled hides, and as their hooves struck soil, the earth shook. Twrch Trwyth threw back his head and bellowed, a sound that split the sky. Then began a devastation that the people of Wales would never forget.

Through Dyfed he charged, fields flattened beneath his weight, cottages smashed into splinters. Fire seemed to follow in his wake as torches were overturned and villagers fled screaming before him. Arthur's war-band landed and gave chase, but the boar was like a storm given flesh, scattering men as though they were dry leaves.

Into Ceredigion the pursuit raged. Arthur's hounds, white-fanged and swift, leapt at the monster's flanks. Their jaws snapped, and their eyes blazed with battle fury. Knights thundered beside them, their lances striking like lightning. Yet each time, Twrch Trwyth shook them off, his tusks cutting down horses, his bristles tearing through mail and flesh alike.

One by one, his sons turned to fight, and each clash shook the hills. Arthur's warriors fell in droves, but the sons of the boar were slain at last. Victory was bought with blood, with so many champions trampled into the mud, beloved knights cast lifeless on the field. The ground ran red, the rivers swelled with gore.

Still the High King pressed on, his face grim, his arm strong. His men fought through terror and grief, driven by their king's unyielding will. The people who watched from the hills would tell their children and their children's children of that sight, of Arthur and his war-band, shining like a river of steel in the sun, chasing a beast that blazed like a demon, tusks dripping, hooves pounding like war-drums, the land itself trembling beneath the fury of the hunt.

At last, in the shadow of the mountains of Glamorgan, the hunt reached its dreadful end. Twrch Trwyth, weary from days of pursuit, at last wheeled about and stood his ground. His eyes glowed like coals in the dark, his bristles stood on end like a forest of spears, and foam dripped from his tusks as though he chewed fire.

Arthur's men formed a ring about him, their shields flashing, their torches casting a circle of firelight on the beast. Spears bristled in every hand, and the king himself sat astride his warhorse at the fore, Excalibur in his grasp. The air was heavy with the scent of sweat, smoke, and blood.

Then the boar bellowed, a sound like the splitting of the heavens, a roar so great that birds fell stunned from the sky and the earth shook beneath their feet. He hurled himself forward, his tusks goring horse and rider alike, scattering Arthur's men like autumn leaves in a storm. Blood spattered the grass, and the screams of men echoed across the valleys.

Yet still the circle closed. Brave warriors leapt at his flanks, clinging to his hide, hacking at his bristled mane with sword and axe. He flung them off, trampling them into the earth, but more came. His hide split under the blades, and at last, through blood and fury, the treasures were glimpsed, glinting among the thick hair of his neck, the great shears and the shining comb, talismans no mortal beast could carry.

With desperate cries, Arthur's champions tore at them, fighting tooth and tusk, until the relics came free. Arthur himself seized them in his gauntleted hands, holding them aloft in triumph. For a heartbeat, the war-band roared with victory.

But Twrch Trwyth was not slain. Maddened with pain, he surged upward with such force that the very ring of iron and fire broke apart. Men scattered, battered and broken, as the boar thundered away into the night, leaving a trail of ruin in his wake.

Arthur, his face bloodied, lifted the comb and shears high. "Enough," he commanded. "We have won what we came for. Let the beast go free, for no man shall ever cage him."

So the hunt ended. The boar, though wounded, fled westward into the wilderness of Cornwall, and the land trembled in his passing. To this day, folk whisper that he still roams the wild hills there, untamed, unbroken, too fierce for any man, even Arthur, to kill.

And when the wind howls through the valleys of Wales, some swear it is the voice of Twrch Trwyth, roaring his defiance against all kings and hunters for eternity.

The Pig, The Cock And The Lamb

A Spanish Tale

This is my own version of a tale written originally as verse by Tomás de Iriarte in his book Literary Fables of Yriarte, published by Ticknor And Fields, London, in 1855.

Tomás de Iriarte (1750–1791) was a Spanish neoclassical poet, playwright, and fabulist best known for his witty and didactic fables written in verse. Born in the Canary Islands and later active in Madrid, Iriarte was deeply influenced by Enlightenment ideals and used his literary work to promote reason, education, and moral instruction.

In old Spain, where the hills of La Mancha roll like sleeping bulls and orange blossoms sweeten the wind, there stood a sun-white farmhouse with a blue-tiled well and a Moorish arch casting shade at noon. In its courtyard lived three companions, Don Tocino, a stout pig the colour of baked clay, Don Gallo, a proud rooster with a comb like a scarlet banner, and Nieves, a lamb as soft as fresh bread, her ears tagged with a bell that chimed like a silver coin.

They were good neighbours, as barnyard folk often are. Don Tocino kept to the coolest corner, where the fig leaves trembled, and practiced the sacred art of the siesta. Don Gallo patrolled the roof tiles and the dung heap like a general, leaping to the well's curb to salute every dawn and every star. Nieves wandered between them, learning the courtyard's songs.

One brass-bright morning, while women beat rugs and a mule dragged the millstone in slow circles, Don Tocino sighed with deep contentment and addressed the lamb. "Ay, niña," he grunted, eyelids drooping, "listen to my philosophy. The world frets and rattles like a peddler's cart, but true happiness is a cool wall, a full belly, and a long nap. Let Fortune dance her fandango, we shall snore through it. Sleep, little cloud, and you will grow."

No sooner had his sermon floated off than Don Gallo fluttered down in a clatter of spurs and pride.

"Caramba!" cried the rooster. "To live is to rise! Stars are the sparks from God's anvil, so who would waste them beneath a blanket? Up with you, little bell, and learn the sky. Before the baker stamps his loaves, before the sexton rings for matins, the wise are already awake. Sleep is rust on the blade."

Nieves' bell tinkled with her worry. Two teachers, two gospels. Which was true? She was a simple lamb, how could she choose?

That night a storm strode over the plain, black as a friar's cloak. The wind pushed at the orange tree, and the well rope thumped. Out of the dark slid Señor Zorra, the fox, as thin as hunger and twice as patient. Don Tocino dreamed on, but Don Gallo's eyes were two embers. He saw the red thread of danger slip beneath the gate.

"¡Al arma!" he trumpeted, a war-cry that shattered the storm. He raked the fox's snout, beat his wings like drums, and rang the courtyard to life. Doors flew open, lanterns bobbed, a shepherd's dog lunged, and Señor Zorra fled, his tail a streak of wet rope, with curses in his throat. Nieves pressed against the wall, heart rattling like dice, and thought, 'Waking saved me.'

The sun returned as tender as cream, and with it came the flamenco-heat of noon. The stones of the courtyard were hot coins, and the air trembled like silk. Nieves, eager to imitate her hero, strutted about in Don Gallo's fashion, eyes wide, chest high. Before long the world blurred at the edges, and her legs, all reeds and pins, wobbled. Don Tocino rolled his eyes, heaved himself to his hooves, and steered her to shade.

"Despacio, niña," he murmured, laying her along the cool wall. He taught her the art of stillness. He schooled her in the art of folding small breath, and how to borrow the stone's patience. Most of all he taught her how to let the heat pass over like a wave. "Not every hour is for trumpets. At noon, the sun eats fools."

Nieves dozed and woke, lived and learned. She rose with stars when the work was to be done, and she slept at noon when the world itself lay down. Some days she kept watch beside Don Gallo, parsing the language of owls and far bells, while on others she leaned against Don Tocino's shoulder and studied the science of rest.

In time, an old arriero, a muleteer with a rosary of road dust and a proverb for each bead, paused at the gate to water his beasts. He watched the pig, the rooster, and the lamb. He listened to the rooster's lectures and the pig's praises of sleep. Then he laughed, as softly as if he were turning pages.

"Cada cual cuenta la feria según le va," he said. "Each tells the tale as he sees it. The rooster loves the stars, so he prescribes the dawn. The pig worships shade, so he anoints the siesta. And the lamb? The lamb must learn which coat fits her weather."

So it was in the sun-white courtyard. Advice flew through the air like swallows, each to its own nest. Don Gallo still saluted the morning with a trumpet's heart, while Don Tocino still taught the wisdom of cool stones and quiet bones. Nieves, bell bright and mind awake, learned to braid both lessons into one good life.

And the old women of the village, who have seen many fairs and many feasts, will tell you still to heed counsel, yes, but wear the habit that suits your soul.

Ned Quayle's Story Of The Fairy Pig

A Manx Tale

This is my own version of a tale written originally by Sophia Morrison in her book Manx Fairy Tales, published by David Nutt, London, in 1911.

Sophia Morrison (1850–1917) was the leading Manx folklorist and cultural activist of the Celtic Revival on the Isle of Man. A tireless collector of tales, songs, and customs, she published the landmark Manx Fairy Tales (1911) and edited the influential cultural journal Mannin (1913–17). As long-serving secretary of Yn Cheshaght Ghailckagh (the Manx Language Society), she organised classes, festivals, and publications that helped sustain Manx Gaelic and promote Manx identity.

When I was a wee lad we lived out by Sloc, where the wind comes straight off the sea and the heather lies across the hills as purple as a king's cloak. Our cottage crouched under the shoulder of the mountain, as snug as a wren in a wall. On the day this happened I was six years old, small enough to slip through a hedge without stirring a thorn.

It was hay-time, and my mother and my granny had gone 'up on the tops' to turn the cut grass while the sun held. "You'll bide quiet," my mother said, tying my scarf. "We'll be home afore the gloamin'. Don't stir from the yard, Ned, my veen."

But the afternoon stretched long, and the gulls cried over the cliffs, and the light slipped from gold to pewter. When the shadows lengthened and still they did not come, a little fear crept in like a draught under a door. I went out, shut the gate behind me, and set off up the mountain path to find them.

I had not gone far when something white flitted across the track. At first I thought it was a neighbour's pig broken loose. But as I looked again, my heart knocked once and then stood listening. This was no ordinary grunter from a byre. It was a pig as snow-white as sea-foam, and its tail was not a twist but a fan, spread like a lady's feather. Its ears were long and lapping, brushing the ling as it ran. Now and again it turned its head, and its eyes, oh, its eyes, burned like live coals raked from a hearth.

"Here, piggy!" I called, as bold as beagles are. I held out my hand. It trotted just beyond my reach, then away, so I ran after it, over the springy turf, past the gorse that pricked my ankles, and along the sheep-walk where the heather hides the stones. The white tail flickered ahead like a beckoning hand. Every few strides it glanced back to make certain I followed.

We climbed and climbed. The wind freshened, and the smell of salt grew keen. A curlew cried, and the light went thin, between the lights, as the old folk say, when the day has not quite died and the night has not quite been born. It is a time for prayer and prudence on our island, for the Mooinjer Veggey, the Little People, take their ease on the paths then, and man should give them the road.

But I was young and full of chase. The white pig ran, and I ran after it, my breath hot in my throat, my feet quick, my hands outstretched. We were higher now, where the grass gives way to stone. The land fell away in a sudden brow, and I came upon it in a rush. One more step and the sea would have had me. Something in me twisted like a rope. I threw myself backward, hands scrabbling, knees skinned, my heart like a trapped bird. At the very lip I heard the pig give a sound, half grunt, half laugh, and stamp its neat white hoof.

Then it came after me.

Down I tore, headlong, stitches stabbing my side, and the creature skimmed the slope behind me as if the rocks were tussocks of ling. I could hear its breath at my heels, as hot as peat-smoke. I could see its shadow doubling mine in the dim light. Our gate loomed up, thank the saints, and I flung myself through and slammed the door, the latch biting home with a click. The white snout struck the wood with a thud that rattled the bolt. Then all was quiet, save for the thundering in my ears.

When at last my mother and my granny came home, they found me as white as drift and shaking. I poured out the tale like milk from a pail. My granny, her hair the colour of cobweb and her eyes as sharp as a wren's, made the sign of the cross and muttered, "A Fairy Pig, as fakin as sheeit ny fainey. The Little People have had their sport with you, Ned. Mind me… never go up the mountain between the lights."

That night I could take no supper. The bread turned to dust in my mouth, and I went to bed as hollow as a reed. Sleep would not have me. I tossed, as hot as an oven, the thoughts in my head like gulls blown in a gale. After a while the latch lifted softly and my mother peeped in to see if I slept.

"Ned, my veen?" she whispered, and in the candle-glow her eyes were like the pig's eyes, ember-red coals under the ash.

A pain stabbed my right leg, sharp and clean, like a thorn driven to the bone. I gasped, and she was gone, and the room was as it had been. But the pain stayed. It rode me like a rider rides a pony, dig-dig with its heels all through the long night. By morning, I could not bear the brush of a sheet. No broth would pass my lips, and I thought I might come apart with it.

On the third day my father said there was no more to be done at home. "We'll take the lad to a Charmer in Castletown," he said. "He has the words and the knowing."

So they lifted me in a sheet, the four of them, one to each corner, and carried me like laundry to the road. They set me in a cart, and never I will never forget the jolting of that journey, the ruts like fists, the wheels like hammers, the whole world knocking at my leg where the pain lived.

The Charmer's house stood in Arbory Street, a plain door with a brass knob that knew many hands. He was a quiet man with eyes like deep water. He looked me over and nodded once. "Leave him," he said. "All of you. I'll do what I can."

So my parents went to wait at The George, and the Charmer took me upstairs himself. He carried me into a small room that smelt of herbs and clean paper. He sent his wife away, set me gently on the floor, and turned the key. Then he took down a great book, as old as a church and as heavy as a conscience, and laid it open beside me. It showed the picture of a little plant, delicate and brave, the sort that grows in cracks where the wind is a tyrant. He pointed to the picture with his left hand, and with his right he traced the sign of the cross upon the sore place where the pain bit like a dog.

Softly, and clear as bell-metal, he said, "I spread this fairy shot in the name of the Father, and of the Son, and of the Holy Ghost, Ned Quayle. If it is a fairy shot, in the name of the Lord, I spread it out of the flesh, out of the sinews, and out of the bones.

At that very moment the pain slipped away like a fish from the hand. One breath I had it, the next breath I did not. I lay blinking, empty and easy, and in its place came a hunger like a tide.

The Charmer's wife brought me to a little table and set a plate before me filled with bread and broth and a bit of cheese. I ate like two boys, as my granny would say, and would have eaten like three if they had let me. The Charmer fetched my father and mother from The George, and when they came in they found me rosy and busy with my spoon.

He spoke to my mother kindly. "No more mountains alone between the lights for the lad," he told her. "Leave a bit of bread on the sill now and again for the Little People. And mind your doors. What we slam in one world may pinch in the other."

We thanked him with what we had, my father's hat in his hands and my mother's eyes wet, and the cart took us home gentler than it came. From that day to this I have been sound, praise God and the good words. But I keep the mark where the stab went through, the skin there as clear as glass to the bone, a round window to a lesson I will not forget.

And if ever you pass our way at Sloc at the coming on of evening, when the sky goes pewter and the first star pricks like a pin, you'll hear the old folk call the children in. For on Mannin we have our manners, and we keep to our paths, and we give the road to those who had it before us. As for white pigs with fan tails, let them run where they will. I, for one, will not follow. Not between the lights. Not ever again.

The Story of the Pigs

An African-American Tale

(As Told By Uncle Remus – an interesting variation on the Three Little Pigs)

This tale is adapted from a story in Joel Chandler Harris' book Nights With Uncle Remus, published by Houghton Mifflin Company, New York & Boston, in 1883.

Joel Chandler Harris (1848–1908) was an American journalist, fiction writer, and folklorist best known for his Uncle Remus stories, a series of African American folktales, fables, and animal stories framed within the character of a kindly, storytelling former slave. Working during the post-Reconstruction era, Harris collected oral tales, many rooted in African, Cherokee, and Southern storytelling traditions, and adapted them into written form using dialect and framed narratives.

Uncle Remus fell quiet again, and the little boy, with nothing better to do, wandered over to the bench where the old man kept his shoemaker's tools. After poking around a bit, he announced, "Looks like you're almost out of bristles."

Uncle Remus sat up, half-cross. "Now what did Miss Sally send you down here for, so you could scatter my things? Don't throw those hog bristles around! There was a time when folks had a hard job getting bristles at all, and who knows when that time might come again? Why, there was even a time when hogs ran down to just one poor little pig, and folks needing bristles had a mighty sorry chance."

His irritation faded as quickly as it came. The boy's eyes lit up. "When was that? How did that happen?"

"I told you that long ago," Uncle Remus said. But the boy insisted he'd never heard it, and kept on until the old man gave in and agreed to tell the story of the pigs.

"Once, way back yonder, an old sow and her children lived among the other animals. As I recall it, the old sow was a widow, and she had five children. Let me see..." Uncle Remus ticked them off with care. "There was Big Pig, Little Pig, Speckle Pig, Blunt, and last and littlest, Runt.

"One day the sow knew her time was near. She called her children and told them they'd soon have to look out for themselves. With what breath she had, she warned them about Brother Wolf, a bad one for sure. 'If you can keep clear of Brother Wolf,' she said, 'you'll be doing mighty well.'

"Big Pig bragged she wasn't scared. Speckle Pig said the same. Blunt claimed he was nearly as big a man as Brother Wolf himself. Runt just nosed around in the straw and grunted. But Widow Sow kept on, 'Mind Brother Wolf. He's mean and deceitful.'

"Not long after, the old sow died, and the children had to fend for themselves. They set to work and each built a house. Big

97

Pig made a brush house. Little Pig built one of sticks. Speckle Pig made a mud house. Blunt put up a plank house. And Runt, she didn't make any fuss or brag, she just worked and built a house of stone.

"By and by, when they were all settled, along came Brother Wolf one morning, licking his chops and wagging his tail. First he came to Big Pig's house. He knocked softly, blim, blim, blim. No answer. Then he knocked hard, blam, blam, blam. Big Pig woke up, came to the door, and asked who was there. Brother Wolf said he was a friend, and sang out:

'If you'll open the door and let me in,

I'll warm my hands and go home again.'

"Big Pig kept asking who it was, so Brother Wolf tried another tack. 'How's your ma?' he asked.

"'My ma is dead,' said Big Pig, 'and before she died she told me to watch out for Brother Wolf. I see you through this crack, and you look a lot like him.'

"Brother Wolf sighed like his feelings were hurt. 'I don't know what turned your ma against me,' he said. 'I heard she was ailing, so I thought I'd drop by and see how the old lady was, and bring her a bag of roasted corn. If your ma were here in her right mind, she'd take these ears and be glad of them, and she'd ask me in to warm my hands by the fire.'

"Well, the talk of roasted corn made Big Pig's mouth water. After a bit more sweet talk, she opened the door and let the wolf in, and bless your soul, that was the last of Big Pig. She didn't have time to squeal or grunt before Brother Wolf gobbled her up.

"The next day Brother Wolf tried the same game with Little Pig. He sang his little song, she let him in, and he 'returned the compliment' by letting her in." Uncle Remus chuckled at his own joke and repeated it, pleased, "Little Pig let Brother Wolf in, and Brother Wolf let Little Pig in. What more can you ask?

"Next time the wolf paid a call, he rapped on Speckle Pig's door and sang:

'If you'll open the door and let me in,

I'll warm my hands and go home again.'

"But Speckle Pig smelled a trick and refused to open. Brother Wolf was a slick talker, though. He asked her to let him just put one paw through the crack. She let the paw in, then he begged for the other paw, then his head, and once his head and paws were in, it took nothing to shove the door and walk right in. It wasn't long before he made fresh meat of Speckle Pig.

"The next day he made away with Blunt. And the day after, he said he'd take a pass at Runt.

"That's where the wolf slipped up. He was like some folks I know. He'd have been smart if he hadn't tried to be too smart. Runt was the smallest of the lot, but the word was out she had good sense like grown folks.

"Brother Wolf crept up to Runt's stone house and sang under the window:

'If you'll open the door and let me in,

I'll warm my hands and go home again.'

"But Runt wouldn't open, and he couldn't break in, because the house was made of stone. After a while he pretended to go away, then came back and knocked, blam, blam, blam!

"Runt sat by the fire, scratched her ear, and called, 'Who's there?'

"'It's Speckle Pig,' the wolf said, somewhere between a snort and a grunt. 'I brought you some peas for your dinner!'

"Runt laughed. 'Sister Speckle Pig never talked through that many teeth,' she said.

"The wolf went off and soon returned to knock again.

"'Who's there?' Runt called.

"'Big Pig,' said the wolf. 'I brought some sweet corn for your supper.'

"Runt peeked through the crack under the door and laughed. 'Sister Big Pig didn't have hair on her hoof.'

"That made the wolf mad. He said he was coming down the chimney. Runt told him that was the only way he could get in. Then, when she heard him scrambling up outside, she piled a big heap of broom-sedge on the hearth. When she heard him coming down inside, she took the tongs and shoved the straw onto the fire. The smoke made Brother Wolf's head swim. He dropped, and before he knew it he was burnt to a crackling. And that was the end of Brother Wolf.

At least," Uncle Remus added carefully, "that was the end of that Brother Wolf."

The old man nodded toward his tool bench. "And that's why you don't waste good hog bristles. Times turn, and you never know when you'll be glad to have what's left."

Old Madge Figgey And The Pig

An English Tale

This tale is adapted from a story told by Robert Hunt in the book Popular Romances of the West of England, published by John Camden Hotten, London, in 1865.

Robert Hunt (1807–1887) was an English scientist and Cornish folklorist whose book Popular Romances of the West of England (1865) became the classic compendium of Cornish legends concerning piskies and mermaids, giants and saints, "knockers" of the mines, charms, drolls, and local superstitions. A pioneer of photochemistry and long-time Keeper of Mining Records at London's Museum of Practical Geology, Hunt straddled industry and imagination: he documented the practices and beliefs of a mining culture he knew firsthand while also writing on science.

In the days when the tin-stamps thudded night and day and the sea-wind sang in the hedges, Madge Figgey lived first at St Leven and later at Burian Church-town. She was a narrow woman in a black shawl, with a stick that knew every stile between cliff and moor. Folks said Madge had a touch of the wise about her, herbs in her basket, a word in Manx or Cornish when storms pressed close, and eyes that could sour milk or sweeten it, according to how you greeted her at the gate.

Next door to her lived Tom Trenoweth, a broad fellow with a temper like a north-easter and, pride of his yard, a fine sow, as sleek and pink as sunrise over Mount's Bay. The creature would root neat as a plough and grow by the hour; Tom called her his "winter bank," meaning he'd feed her up against the cold and the lean months.

One bright morning Madge leaned on Tom's wall and watched the sow turning up the garden as if counting coins.

"Tom," she said, mild as milk, "what will you take for the pig?"

"A pound's the worth of her," replied Tom, tightening his mouth.

"I'll give five shillings," says Madge, and taps the basket with her stick.

Tom laughed, not kindly. "I'll not sell her to you nor to any man. I'm bringing her into the house to fatten for myself against winter."

Madge nodded, as slow as a prayer, and wagged her finger. "You'll wish you had, Tom Trenoweth."

From that very day the sow ceased to goody, that's what the old folk say when a beast no longer thrives. The more corn Tom fed her, the leaner she turned. Her back rose as sharp as a slate ridge, and her sides sounded as hollow as a gorse stem in wind.

Madge came by again, stick tapping the stones. "Will 'ee sell her now, Tom?"

"No, and be hanged to you," growled Tom.

"Arreah, Tom," said Madge, "you'll wish you had afore the week is out."

By the week's end the sow was skin and bone, yet she ate as if for three. Tom could stomach it no longer. "Market, then," he swore, "and fetch what she'll fetch." He tied a rope about her leg, more for show than need, for the poor creature could hardly stand, and set off on the Penzance road.

No sooner had they reached the highroad than the sow changed. She pricked her ears, drew a breath like a bellows, and ran. Not a pig's scamper, mind, but thin and straight like a greyhound, over hedges and ditches, across the lane, then through Leah Lanes, so fleet the puddles hardly had time to ripple. Tom clung to the rope till his arm near left its socket, stumbling and swearing, dragged along like a tin-worker's sack behind a cart. He was soon fair out of breath and had to drop the rope. The sow, gentle as a lamb now, trotted on, but only where it pleased her.

Past furze and furrow they went till they came to Tregenebris Downs, where the road forks, one way to Sancreed, the other to Penzance. "I'll have you market-ward yet," muttered Tom, catching the rope again and turning her toward Penzance.

The moment her feet touched the market-road, the sow bolted. The rope jerked out of Tom's hand, off she went, as fast as a squall, and never stopped till she slipped herself under Tregenebris Bridge, which is less a bridge than a long stone bolt, a drain-tunnel tightest in the middle. In she went, and midway she stuck fast. She couldn't go forward, and she wouldn't come back. Her grunts boomed in the stone like a smugglers' secret.

Tom raged awhile. He threw every stone he could find, first at her head, then at her tail. He got for his pains only a grunt and a puff of dust. Time went like tide. He had eaten nothing since five in the morning, and his belly was as hollow as a conch. At last, with the sun slanting red and his temper spent, Tom cursed the day and the pig both, and turned to tramp home.

Who should come along then but old Madge Figgey, shawl tight, stick in one hand, basket in the other.

"Why, Tom, is that you? What are you doing out here at this hour?"

Tom jabbed a finger at the bridge. "If you've a mind to know, look under there. I'm damned if I can tell the rest."

Madge bent her head. "Aye, I hear her grunting. What'll you sell her for now?"

"If you can get her out, take her!" said Tom. "Only, have you anything to eat? I'm starving."

Madge opened her basket and passed him a twopenny loaf.

"Thank you kindly," said Tom, tearing it in his teeth. "Now, devil take the both of you!"

Madge didn't answer Tom. She went to the mouth of the bolt and tapped three times with her stick, as lightly as a wren pecking. Then she spoke, as softly as foam on sand, words as old as the moor. No one standing by could swear what tongue it was, Cornish maybe, or older still.

Then, clear as a bell, she called, "Cheat! Cheat! Cheat!"

At the first "Cheat," the sow snorted. At the second, she wriggled. At the third, with a heave and a squeal, she slipped free, shook herself like rain off a hedge, and trotted out neat as you please. She went to Madge's heels as if she'd a collar on and followed her home like a dog.

Tom stood staring, crumbs on his shirtfront, rope limp in his fist. Madge only nodded as she passed him and said, as if discussing weather, "Best mind your bargains, Tom Trenoweth. Winter comes, and so do words."

They say the sow fattened properly at Madge Figgey's, and none could say how. Some swore it was nothing but kindly scraps and clean water, while others said there were charms under the hearthstone and herbs steeped by a new moon in a Penzance bottle. As for Tom, he told the tale often enough in the inns from Sancreed to Newlyn, but when people laughed he would only shake his head and say, "She warned me. I wish I had."

And if you pass Tregenebris Bridge at sundown, you'll still hear, perhaps, a grunt under the stone and the tap of a stick on granite, like rain that knows your name. Mind your tongue with the wise folk, and weigh your offers fair, else your luck may run as lean as a sow on market day, till someone else calls it out with "Cheat! Cheat! Cheat!"

Why the Warthog Walks on His Knees

A South African (Zulu / Nguni) Story

This tale is my own versions of a traditional African legend taken from various sources in my own collection of folk and fairy tales. Why the Warthog Walks on His Knees belongs to the broad category of "pourquoi tales" ("why" stories) that explain the distinctive traits of animals.

Tales like this were passed down orally across Southern Africa as moral lessons for children, warning against vanity, arrogance, or disobedience, while also giving colourful explanations for the odd appearances of animals.

Long ago, in the days when all animals still walked tall and proud, Warthog was the handsomest of beasts. His back was straight, his legs long, and his head high. His tusks gleamed like ivory, polished bright by the grasses he chewed. Even Lion, king of the savanna, admitted that Warthog had a noble bearing.

But Warthog had one fault, greater than any other, and that was his pride. He strutted before the other creatures, tossing his head so the sun would flash on his tusks, saying, "Look at me. See how fine my stance is! Look how sharp my tusks are! Who among you could match me?"

The animals grew weary of his boasting. Even little Hare, quick-tongued and mischievous, snapped one day, "Warthog, you may be tall, but your shadow is longer than your sense."

Warthog only laughed. "What need have I for sense? I have tusks!"

Then , one hot season, when water grew scarce, Warthog came to drink at the last pool left on the plain. There he found Leopard, already lapping at the edge.

"Step aside," said Warthog, puffing out his chest. "This pool belongs to me. Do you not see my tusks?"

Leopard snarled, "We all thirst, and no beast owns the water. Share, or there will be blood."

But Warthog would not listen. "You think your spots make you fine? My tusks are sharper than your claws. My stance is prouder than your slinking. I will not share with the likes of you."

The animals who had gathered at the pool murmured, anger rising among them. Even gentle Antelope stamped her hoof. "Enough, Warthog! Your tusks may be sharp, but your heart is dull."

Still Warthog boasted. Still he refused to bow his head.

That night, the ancestors stirred. From the dark sky came a voice carried on the wind. "Pride has no place in the herd. Pride tramples the grass, drinks the water, and leaves none for the rest."

When dawn came, the animals saw Warthog changed. His legs were bent beneath him, and he could no longer stand tall. To drink, he had to kneel. To feed, he had to bend his face low to the dust. His tusks, once flashing proudly toward the sky, now jutted awkwardly toward the ground.

Warthog groaned. "What has been done to me?"

And the wind answered, "Until you learn humility, you will walk on your knees. Let every bite of grass remind you of the dust you came from."

From that day to this, warthogs no longer strut proudly on long legs. They kneel in the dust, their faces close to the earth, their tusks scraping the ground. And when they drink, they do so quickly, darting away before others can scold them.

The other animals laugh, but not cruelly, for they know the story well. "Look," they say to their children, "see how Warthog walks on his knees. Remember, pride will always bow you down."

Ass Or Pig

A Japanese Tale

This tale is adapted from a story told by Rachel Harriette Busk in her book Roman Legends: A Collection Of The Fables And Folk-Lore Of Rome, published by Estes And Lauriat, Boston, in 1877.

Rachel Harriette Busk was a 19th-century British folklorist, translator, and travel writer who helped introduce Continental and "Far Eastern" tale traditions to English readers. Busk paired lively retellings with notes on customs, proverbs, festivals, and beliefs, creating early, influential English-language snapshots of regional oral traditions, sometimes romanticised by Victorian taste, but still valued as rich records of 19th-century folk culture.

A countryman was going along driving a pig before him. "Let's have a bit of fun with that fellow," said the brother porter of a monastery to the father guardian, as they saw him coming along the road. "I'll call his pig an ass, and of course he'll say it's a pig. Then I shall laugh at him for not knowing better, and he will grow angry. Then I'll say, 'Well, will you have the father guardian to settle the dispute? And if he decides I'm right I shall keep the beast for myself.' Then you come and say it is an ass, and we'll keep it."

The father guardian agreed, with a hearty laugh, and as soon as the countryman came up the brother porter did all as he had arranged.

The countryman was so sure of his case that he willingly submitted to the arbitration of the father guardian, but great was his dismay when the father guardian decided against him, and he had to go home without his pig.

But what did the countryman do? He dressed himself up as a poor girl, and about nightfall, with a storm coming on, he rang the doorbell of the monastery and asked for the charity of shelter for the night.

'Impossible!' said the brother porter, " We can't have any womenkind in here."

"But the dark, and the storm!" clamoured the pretended girl, "think of that. You can't leave me out here all alone."

"I'm very sorry," said the porter, "but the thing's impossible. I can't do it."

The good father guardian, hearing the dispute at that unusual hour, put his head out of the window and asked what it was all about.

"It is a difficult case, brother porter," he said when he had heard the girl's request. "If we take her in we infringe our rule in one way, but if we leave her exposed to every kind of peril we sin against its spirit in another direction. I only see one way out of it. I can't send her into any of your cells, but I will let her pass the night in mine, provided she is content not to undress, and will consent to sit up in a chair."

This was exactly what the countryman wanted, therefore he gave a ready assent, and the father guardian took him up into his cell. The pretended girl sat up in a chair quietly enough through the dark of the night, but when morning began to dawn, out came a stick that had been hidden under the petticoats, and whack, whack, a fine drubbing the poor father guardian got to the tune of, "So you think I don't know a pig from an ass, do you?"

When he had bruised him all over, the countryman made the best of his way downstairs, and off and away he was before anyone could catch him.

The next day what did he do? He dressed up like a doctor, and came round asking if anyone had any ailments to cure.

"That's just the thing for us," said the brother porter to himself as he saw him come by. "The father guardian was afraid to let the usual doctor attend him, for fear of the scandal of the story coming out. This strange doctor will just do, as there is no need to tell him anything."

The countryman in his new disguise, therefore, was taken up to the father guardian's cell.

"There's nothing very much the matter," he said when he had examined the wounds and bruises. "It might all be set right in a day by a certain herb," which he named.

The herb was a difficult one to find, but as it was so important to get the father guardian cured immediately, before any inquiry should be raised as to the cause of his sufferings, the whole community set out to wander over the Campagna in search of it.

As soon as they were a good way off, the pretended doctor took out a thick stick which he held concealed under his long robe, and whack, whack, he beat the poor father guardian more terribly even than before, to the tune of, "So you think I don't know an ass from a pig, do you?"

The father guardian's cries were so piteous that they all of the searching brothers returned from their search in haste, but not till the countryman had made good his escape.

"We have sinned, my brethren," said the father guardian when they were all gathered round him, "and I have suffered justly for it. We had no right to take the man's pig, even for a joke. Let it now, therefore, be restored to him, and in amends let's give him an ass also."

So the countryman got his pig back, and a donkey into the bargain.

The Pig's Head Soothsayer

A Mongolian Tale

This tale is adapted from a story told by Rachel Harriette Busk in her book Sagas from the Far East, published by Griffith and Farran, London, in 1873.

An often unappreciated aspect of Busk's work is that she did urban fieldwork long before it was fashionable. Living for years in Rome, she gathered Roman folklore directly from nursemaids, market women, artisans, and contadine, often noting snippets of dialect, charms, counting-out rhymes, and saints' legends verbatim, and sometimes crediting individual tellers, which was unusual for the era. In her notes she then cross-mapped those Roman items to Tyrolean, Spanish, and "Far Eastern" analogues, essentially doing early motif-comparison work decades before Aarne–Thompson indexing became standard.

Long ago, a man and his wife lived on the edge of a prosperous kingdom. The wife was a capable housekeeper who managed their fields and herds. The husband was dull and lazy. He ate, drank, and slept from sunrise to sunrise. At last the wife could bear it no longer. "Stop idling," she told him. "Get up, be a man, and find work. Your father's inheritance is almost gone, so you must find some way to make it last."

When he weakly asked, "What should I do?" she answered, "How could I know that for you? At least get up and try. Go look around and see what you can find." And she went back to the fields.

After many days of the same talk, the man finally went out. He did not plan or think, he simply did as she said and looked around. He came to a place where a clan of herdsmen had recently camped, and saw a fox, a dog, and a bird fighting over something. When he stepped closer, they scattered in fear, and he found what they'd been battling for, which was a sheep's stomach filled with butter. He took it home and stored it away. When his wife asked where it came from, he told her he'd found it where the herders had been.

"Well, it's a fine thing to be a man!" she said scornfully. "I can work all day and not make as much, but you go out one day in your whole life for a single moment, and come back with riches."

Encouraged by her words, the man began to think he could do even better. "Give me a good horse, proper clothes, a dog, and a bow and arrows," he said. "Then you'll see what I can do."

Glad to hear some resolve at last, the wife hurried to equip him. She gave him what he asked for, added a thick felt cloak against the rain and a cap for his head, helped him mount, and slung the bow over his shoulder.

He rode across wide plains with no purpose and no sense of direction and met no living soul for many days. At last, on the

115

great steppe, he spotted a fox in the distance. "Ha," he said, "one of my friends from last time. No sheep's paunch of butter today, but if I can kill him, his skin will make a warm cap."

He had never learned to shoot, so the bow was useless. He urged his horse after the fox, but the fox ran faster and darted into a marmot hole.

"I've got you now!" the man said. He dismounted, stripped off all his clothes to move more freely, and tied them to the saddle. He tied the dog to the bridle and stuffed his cap into the mouth of the burrow. Then he lifted a heavy stone and pounded the ground to crush the fox.

Frightened by the blows, the fox burst from the hole so hard it carried the cap away on its head. The dog lunged after it, and the horse, tied to the dog, had to follow, and off they went, horse, dog, clothes, and all his belongings, while the man lay on the ground with not a stitch to his name.

He wandered on and came to a river marking the border of a powerful khan's realm. Slipping into the khan's stable, he burrowed under the straw and covered himself completely. There he warmed up and rested.

As he lay hidden, the khan's beautiful daughter came out to take the air. Before going back inside, she dropped the khan's talisman, a jewel-charm said to preserve his life, and walked on without noticing. Though the thing was precious both for its gems and its protection of the khan, the man was too lazy to get up and pick it up. He let it lie.

After sunset the herds returned. The cow-girl swept the yard without seeing the talisman, and it was tossed onto the dung heap. The man saw that too, and still did not move.

The next day the place was in an uproar. The khan sent messengers far and wide, announcing the loss of his talisman and promising a reward to whoever returned it. He had the great trumpet sounded, the one blown only when the laws of the realm were proclaimed, and summoned all the wise men and diviners to locate the talisman by their arts.

The man, under the straw, heard it all and did nothing. At dawn, stable hands came to lay down fresh bedding and found him. "Out with you!" they shouted. Forced at last to move, he thought of the talisman. When they asked who he was, he said, "I'm a soothsayer. I have come to divine where the khan's talisman lies."

They told the khan. "But he has no clothes," they added. The khan sent garments for him and ordered them to bring the soothsayer in.

Before the khan, the man was asked what he needed to perform his divination. "Bring me a pig's head," he said, "a piece of five-coloured silk, and a large baling-cake."

These were provided. He set the pig's head on a wooden stand, draped it with the silk, and put the cake in its mouth. Then he sat facing it, as if in deep contemplation.

On the third day, the day named in the proclamation, people gathered from everywhere. Wrapped in a long mantle like a dream-diviner, he sat before the pig's head and seemed to question it as people filed past. To each he acted as if receiving an answer, "The talisman is not with this one," and

"Not with that one," which pleased many, eager to be declared innocent.

At last he ended that part of the rite. "The talisman is not in anyone's possession," he pronounced. "Now we will divine by the earth."

He walked the circuit of the khan's dwelling, pausing as if consulting the pig's head, until he came to the dung heap. Assuming a solemn posture, he said, "Here, somewhere, the khan's talisman will be found." He turned the heap over and brought the talisman to light.

The people cried out in wonder, "The Pig's-Head Diviner has worked wonders!"

The khan called him. "How shall I reward you for restoring my talisman?" he asked.

The man, who never thought beyond the present moment, said, "Give me my clothes, horse, fox, dog, and bow and arrows, the ones I lost."

The khan marvelled that he asked for nothing more. "A strange soothsayer," he said. "Still, give him those, and two elephants loaded with meal and butter besides."

So they loaded him with all he asked and more, and escorted him home.

His wife saw him coming from far off and brought out brandy to meet him. When she saw the elephants with their loads, her eyes widened, but knowing he liked peace, she asked no questions that night. In the morning she made him tell her everything before they rose. When she heard the smallness of his request after such a service, she said, "If a man means to be called a man, he should know how to use an opportunity."

Then she sat down and wrote a letter in his name to the khan: "While your life-talisman was briefly in my hands, I discerned that Your Majesty suffers from a bodily affliction. It was to draw this out that I asked for the dog and the fox. What reward the khan grants for this further service is for the khan to decide."

She took the letter herself to the khan. Pleased to think the soothsayer was curing a malady he had not known about, the khan sent her back with two more elephant-loads of treasure. From then on, they had enough to live in comfort.

Now, the khan had once had six brothers. Long ago the seven had gone out to amuse themselves and, in a thick wood, saw a maiden of astonishing beauty playing with a he-goat. They stood and stared until they were tired of standing, though never tired of looking. "Where do you come from, beautiful maiden?" one asked.

"I followed this he-goat here," she said.

"Will you come with us seven brothers and be our wife?" asked the first speaker. She agreed and went home with them.

But the maiden and the goat were man-eaters in disguise. The male manggus had taken the form of a he-goat, while the female manggus had taken the form of a beautiful girl. Each year they devoured the life of one brother. Now only the khan remained, and they had begun to consume his life as well.

The ministers, seeing the brothers dead and the khan failing despite every remedy and physician, held council. "We have one way left," they said. "Send for the Pig's-Head Soothsayer who found the talisman. Let him restore the khan." They all agreed and dispatched four horsemen to fetch him.

When they explained the matter, the man was embarrassed and had no idea what to say. His vacant look passed for deep meditation, and their respect for him grew. His wife told them to stable their horses and stay the night. In the dark she asked her husband what they wanted, and he told her.

"Last time you stirred yourself and luck favoured you," she said. "You've sat like a stump ever since, so who knows how you'll do now? Still, you must go if the khan has sent for you."

In the morning he told the messengers, "In the night I saw how to help the khan. I will come with you."

He wrapped himself in a mantle, combed his hair over the crown, took a large bead-string in his left hand, tied the five-coloured silk around his right arm, and set off carrying the pig's head.

At the khan's palace, the two manggus were alarmed by his strange appearance and his reputation, and they feared that he truly knew them. He set a baling-cake as big as a man at the head of the khan's bed, put the pig's head atop it, and sat facing it, murmuring incantations. Convinced he was dangerous, the manggus withdrew to confer. Deprived of their presence, the khan's pain eased and he fell into a deep, peaceful sleep. The attendants took this as a sign of cure and left the soothsayer in full charge.

Free from watchful eyes, the man stole a look at the sleeping khan. The depth of the sleep frightened him, for surely the khan must be dying. He tried to wake him, calling, "Great Khan! Mighty Khan!" The khan did not stir. Certain that he was dead, the man decided he must run. But the first open doorway was the treasury, and the guards shouted, "Stop thief!"

He bolted into the storehouse; again, "Stop thief!"

At last he ducked into the stable, only to find the he-goat at the door. Afraid of its horns, he forced himself to creep behind, leapt onto its back, and struck its head three times. In a flash, swift as a column of blue smoke driven straight by wind, the goat shot off toward the khanin's quarters, throwing the man to the ground. He scrambled up and ran after it and heard the goat speaking inside with the khanin.

"The Pig's-Head Soothsayer is a soothsayer indeed," said the goat. "He divined I was in the stable. Then he mounted me and hit me three mighty blows. He knows our weight. We must flee."

"I agree," said the khanin. "I saw at once he recognised us. Fortune has left us. If we stay, we perish. I know what he will do. In a day or two, when he has cured the khan by keeping us from devouring his life, he will assemble all the men with weapons and all the women with faggots for burning. He will have them bring you bound before him and command you to drop your disguise. You will have to obey. Once you stand in your true shape, they will cut and shoot you and burn your body. Then they will do the same to me. Therefore, tomorrow or the next day, we must slip away."

Hearing this, the soothsayer needed no more. He returned confidently to his place by the pig's head.

121

In the morning the khan woke refreshed. "The soothsayer's power has weakened my illness," he said. "If that is so," the soothsayer answered, "and if the khan trusts his servant, command that all subjects gather, the men with weapons, the women each with a bundle of wood."

The khan gave the order. When everyone had assembled, the soothsayer set up the pig's head and commanded that the he-goat be brought from the stable, bound and saddled. He mounted, struck the goat three times with all his strength, dismounted, and shouted with all his voice, "Lay aside your assumed form!"

Before all eyes the goat became a hideous manggus. With swords, lances, sticks, and stones, the people fell upon it and crippled it. Then they burned it to death.

"Now bring the khanin," the soothsayer said. They dragged her down amid jeers. With one hand on the pig's head, as if taking authority from it, he cried, "Resume your true form!"

She too became a monstrous manggus, and they put her to death like the first.

The soothsayer rode back to the palace through a throng of people bowing and praising him, some strewing barley, some bringing gifts. It took him nearly a full day to reach the khan. The khan welcomed him gratefully and asked what he wanted as reward.

The man replied in his simple way, "In our region we have none of the wooden pegs you put in oxen's noses. Give me a quantity of those to take home."

The khan ordered up three sacks of nose-pegs, and seven elephants loaded with meal and butter besides.

When the man arrived, his wife came out with brandy. She praised him on seeing the seven elephants, but when she learned how he had saved the khan, she was angry he had asked so little and resolved to go herself the next day.

She went disguised and sent in a letter, saying, "Though I, the Pig's-Head Soothsayer, brought the khan back from his illness, a trace of it remains. It was to remove this that I asked for the ox-nose pegs. What reward is due for this further service the khan will judge."

"The man speaks truth," the khan said after reading. "Let him, his wife, parents, and friends all come live with me."

When they came, the khan said, "To send a benefactor away with gifts is not enough. That I was not killed by the manggus is your doing. That the kingdom did not fall is your doing. That my ministers were not devoured is your doing. Therefore we will share the inheritance and rule equally."

He gave the man half the realm and rich appointments to all his kin. Thus the wife became khanin, free at last from the burden of field and flock, while her husband continued to live as idly as before.

The Carving of Mac Datho's Boar

An Irish Tale

This tale is adapted from a story told by Thomas William Hazen Rolleston in his book The High Deeds of Fin and Other Bardic Romances of Ancient Ireland, published by Williams and Norgate, London, in 1892.

Thomas William Hazen Rolleston (1857–1920) was an Irish writer, poet, and critic associated with the Irish Literary Revival, best known for shaping Celtic lore for general readers. A founder of the Irish Literary Society in London, he edited and wrote for literary journals and produced elegant prose retellings that became entry points to Irish mythology. Beyond Celtic material he wrote literary criticism and biographies and translated from, helping bridge European letters and the emerging modern Irish canon.

Once, in the green province of Leinster, there lived a generous lord named Mesroda mac Datho. Two treasures made his name famous across Ireland. He possessed a hound faster than any dog or wild beast in Éire, and a boar so huge and splendid that no one had ever seen its like.

News of the hound ran ahead of riders and wind. Soon Conor, king of Ulster, and Maev, queen of Connacht, each sent messengers asking to buy the dog. By chance both envoys reached mac Datho's fort on the very same day.

The Connacht messenger spoke first, saying, "For the hound we'll pay six hundred milch cows, plus a chariot with two fine horses, the best in Connacht. In a year, we'll double it."

Ulster's envoy bowed. "We'll match any price Connacht offers, and grant Ulster's friendship and alliance. That's worth more than silver or cattle."

Mac Datho said nothing. For three days he neither ate nor drank. At night he faced the wall and tossed like a net in a storm. His wife noticed and sat beside him.

"Food's at your elbow, and still you fast," she said. "You turn away from me at night, and sleep won't have you. What's gnawing at you?"

Mac Datho muttered an old, sour proverb, "Never trust a thrall with money, or a woman with a secret."

She snorted. "And when should a man speak to a woman if not when something's wrong? What your mind can't mend, another's might."

So he told her that both Ulster and Connacht wanted the hound. "If I refuse either one," he said, "they'll raid my herds and kill my people."

"Then listen," she said. "Give the hound to both, and tell both to come fetch him. If there's raiding to be done, let them raid each other. But do not keep the hound."

At that, mac Datho stood, shook off his gloom, called for food and drink, and laughed with his guests. In secret he told Connacht's messenger, "I'll give the hound to Queen Maev.

Fetch him on such-and-such a day with your nobles. I'll host you royally."

Connacht's man left, delighted.

To Ulster's envoy he said the same, only swapping names. "I'll give the hound to King Conor. Come on that same day with your champions. You'll be welcomed as befits you."

When the appointed day came, the flower of Ulster and Connacht crowded before mac Datho's fort. Conor was there, and Ailill, Maev's husband. Mac Datho met them at the gate. "Welcome, warriors," he said, "though we weren't quite set for two armies at once."

He led them into the great hall. It had seven doors, and between every two doors were benches for fifty men. The men of Ulster and Connacht didn't look on each other as dinner guests. For three hundred years their provinces had found reasons to fight.

"Kill the great boar," mac Datho ordered, and it was done. For seven years the boar had drunk the milk of fifty cows. Better it had drunk poison, some said later, given the trouble that came from carving it.

When the boar was roasted, servants carried it in, shining, crackling, and huge. Bowls and platters followed in a train. "If you find the feast lacking," mac Datho said, "we'll slaughter more before morning."

"The boar is good," said King Conor.

"A fine beast," said Ailill. "Now, mac Datho, how shall we divide it?"

There lounged in Ulster's ranks a man named Bricriu, son of Carbad, silver-tongued, sharp-toothed, famous for stirring trouble, but he never fought himself. He called across the hall, "How else would you divide a champion's meat but by giving it to whoever is greatest in deeds? Here are Ireland's best. Haven't any of us put a fist across the others' noses before?"

"Good," said Ailill. "So be it."

"We agree," said Conor. "We've lads here who've walked the borders more than once."

"You'll need them tonight," growled an old Connacht warrior. "Often we've seen them flat on their backs on the roads of rushy Dedah, leaving fat steers with us for pay."

"Once you had a fat bullock indeed," answered Moonremar of Ulster. "Your own brother. He came by the rushy road of Conlad and never went back."

"A better man than him fell at Tara Luachra," said Lugad of Munster. "Irloth, son of Fergus mac Leda, by Echbael's hand."

"Echbael?" barked Keltchar, son of Uthecar Hornskin of Ulster. "I took his head."

So it went on, with boasts traded like spear-throws. Finally Ket son of Maga of Connacht strode to the boar, drew the carving knife, and lifted his voice. "Let one man of Ulster match me, or hold your tongues and let me carve!"

Silence followed. Then Conor whispered to Logary the Triumphant, "Stand for us."

Logary rose. "Ket shall not carve for us all."

"Not so quick," said Ket. "In Ulster, boys prove themselves on us. You came to the border once. I took your chariot and horses and left my spear through your ribs. Sit down." Logary sat.

"Ket shall never divide that pig," cried a tall, fair Ulsterman, striding forward.

"Who's this?" said Ket.

"Angus, son of Lama Gabad," shouted the Ulstermen.

"And why is his father called 'Hand-Lacking'?" Ket smiled thinly. "He cast a spear at me. I cast it back. His hand lay on the field. Shall his son measure himself with me?" Angus sat.

"Keep the contest going," Ket taunted, "or I'll cut."

"You won't," thundered another. "Owen Mór, King of Fermag."

"I remember you," said Ket. "I lifted a herd from your very door. You put a spear through my shield. I sent it back and took an eye. One-eyed you are still." Owen sat.

"Anyone else?" Ket asked.

"Moonremar, son of Gerrkind," came the call.

"Three days ago," said Ket, "I carried three heads from your fort. One was your firstborn." Moonremar sat.

"Mend, son of Sword-heel," the Ulstermen cried.

"I named your father," Ket laughed. "I cut his heel, and off he went with only one. What brings his son here?" Mend sat.

A huge, grey Ulsterman rose. "Keltchar, son of Uthecar."

"Steady, Keltchar," said Ket. "Once I raided to your very gate. In a narrow pass we traded spears. Mine went through your loins. You've not been the same since." Keltchar sat.

"Who else?" Ket called. "Or do I carve?"

Up rose Cuscrid the Stammerer, son of King Conor.

"He has a king's makings," Ket nodded. "No thanks to you," snapped Cuscrid.

"You made your first foray on our borders," said Ket. "You left a third of your men. You rode away with my spear through your throat. The sinews never healed, and that's why you're called the Stammerer." Cuscrid sat.

So Ket shamed all Ulster in turn. No one else answered.

He lifted the knife, triumphant. And then came the sound of hoofbeats, and shouting, and the hall doors were thrown wide. The Ulstermen roared. Down the centre strode Conall Cernach, Conall of the Victories. King Conor sprang up, tore the helmet from his head, and shouted for joy.

"Glad am I," Conall called, "to find a feast ready. Who carves the boar?"

"Ket son of Maga," they answered. "No one could win the Champion's Portion from him."

"Is that so, Ket?" said Conall.

"It is," said Ket. "And welcome, Conall, iron-hearted, frost-bright, ever-victorious. Hail, son of Finnchoom!"

"Hail to you, Ket," said Conall, smiling. "Flower of heroes, lord of chariots, bull in battle. Rise and give me place."

"Why should I?" Ket asked.

"Do you want a contest?" said Conall. "You shall have it. By the gods I swear since I first took up weapons, not a day has passed I didn't fell a Connachtman, and not a night I didn't raid them; I never slept without a Connachtman's head beneath my knee."

Ket bowed his head. "You are the better man. I yield you the boar. Yet if my brother Anluan were here, he'd match you deed for deed. I grieve he is not."

"Anluan is here," said Conall, and drew from his belt Anluan's head, flinging it into Ket's face.

Steel sang out of its sheaths. Benches overturned. Warriors rushed the doors and the hall exploded into battle. The fight spilled into the field. Connacht broke and ran. Mac Datho's hound raced with the Ulstermen, caught Ailill's chariot, and locked its jaws on the pole. The charioteer chopped, and the hound's head fell, but its jaws clamped so tight that when Ailill halted, the head still gripped the pole. They named that place Íbar Cinn Chon, the Yew of the Hound's Head.

As Conor pressed hard after Ailill, the Connacht charioteer Ferloga slipped into the heather. When Conor thundered past, Ferloga sprang up and seized him by the throat.

"What do you want?" Conor gasped.

"End the chase," said Ferloga. "Take me to Emain Macha. While I'm there, let the maidens of Ulster sing me a serenade each night."

"Done," said Conor. He brought Ferloga to Emain, kept him a year, and then escorted him as far as Athlone with gifts of two fine horses with golden bridles. As for the serenade, well, the horses sang more sweetly than the maidens ever did.

And that is how a hound, a boast, and a boar turned a feast into a battle, and why a yew by the roadside is still called the Hound's Head. As for mac Datho, he gave his dog to both provinces, and they did the harrying for him, just as his wife advised.

Why the Pig's Snout Is Flat

A West African (Yoruba / Efik) Story

This tale is my own versions of a traditional African legend taken from various sources in my own collection of folk and fairy tales. Why the Pig's Snout Is Flat belongs to the family of African pourquoi tales, stories that explain why an animal looks or behaves the way it does.

This particular one is most often found in West African oral traditions, especially among the Yoruba (Nigeria) and the Efik/Ibibio (southeastern Nigeria / Cameroon) peoples. In these stories, pigs (which were not native to Africa until introduced, but quickly became a part of village life) are given folktale "origin" explanations for their flat snouts.

In the beginning, when the world was still young, the animals all lived much as people do. They spoke with voices as clear as yours or mine, they gathered in markets, they argued, they laughed, and they quarrelled.

In those days, Pig was very proud of his nose. It was long and round, with a fine sharp point. He would strut through the village showing it off, boasting,

"Look at me! With this noble snout, I can sniff out the sweetest yams, the fattest roots, the juiciest cassava! No one has a nose like mine!"

The other animals rolled their eyes.

Goat muttered, "Boast, boast, boast. He talks more than he eats."

But trickster Anansi pricked up his ears. Anansi loved nothing more than humbling the proud, and Pig's pride was as fat as his belly. So Anansi thought to himself, Let us see how long that fine nose lasts when I have had my fun.

So, one day, as Pig snuffled about the forest, Anansi crept close and whispered, "Friend Pig, with that wonderful snout of yours, you could dig up treasures the rest of us cannot reach."

Pig puffed out his chest. "Of course I could! I am the master of the earth itself!"

"Well then," Anansi said slyly, "deep in the earth there is a yam as long as a canoe and as sweet as honey. Only you, with that perfect nose, could find it. Dig, and it will be yours."

Pig's eyes shone. Without a thought, he plunged his snout into the earth. He dug and dug, rooting and shoving, while Anansi chuckled. Pig pushed harder and harder, convinced that the treasure yam was just below his snout.

But there was no yam, only hard earth and stones. Pig's nose scraped and scraped, pressing flatter and flatter as he shoved it against the ground.

At last Pig raised his head, snout bloody and swollen, no longer proud and sharp but squashed flat against his face.

133

Anansi burst out laughing so hard he nearly rolled into the bushes.

"Where is the yam?" Pig cried, bewildered.

"Why, you've already eaten it!" Anansi teased, pointing at Pig's ruined nose. "Look how much earth you swallowed while you rooted about! A finer feast you'll never find."

Pig groaned, but the other animals gathered round and laughed, too. Goat bleated, Monkey shrieked, even the birds in the trees cackled. Poor Pig slunk away, his snout ruined forever.

And from that day to this, Pig's children and children's children have all borne the same flat nose, good for nothing but rooting in the soil. That is why you see them still, snuffling and grunting in the earth, searching for yams and roots they may never find.

The Sheep And The Pig Who Set Up House

A Norwegian Tale

This tale is adapted from a story told by Peter Christen Asbjørnsen in his book Tales from the Fjeld, published by Chapman & Hall, London, in 1874.

Peter Christen Asbjørnsen (1812–1885) was a Norwegian folklorist, writer, and naturalist who, with his friend Jørgen Moe, created the landmark collections Norske Folkeeventyr and Norske huldre-eventyr og folkesagn, the classic "Asbjørnsen & Moe" tales. Traveling rural Norway in the 1830s–40s, they recorded oral storytellers and shaped the narratives into vivid, idiomatic prose that helped forge a national literary style during Norway's romantic-national revival. Many globally beloved stories come from their collections.

Once on a time there was a sheep who stood in the pen to be fattened, so he lived well, and was stuffed and crammed with everything that was good. So it went on, till, one day, the dairymaid came and gave him still more food, and then she said, "Eat away, sheep. You won't be much longer here. We are going to kill you tomorrow."

It is an old saying, that women's counsel is always worth having, and that there is a cure and physic for everything but death. "But, after all," said the sheep to himself, "there may be a cure even for death this time."

So he ate till he was ready to burst; and when he was crammed full, he butted out the door of the pen, and took his way to the neighbouring farm. There he went to the pigsty to a pig whom he had known out on the common, and ever since had been the best friends with.

"Good day!" said the sheep, "and thanks for our last merry meeting."

"Good day," answered the pig, "and the same to you."

"Do you know," said the sheep, "why it is you are so well off, and why it is they fatten you and take such pains with you?"

"No, I don't," said the pig.

"Many a flask empties the cask, I suppose you know that," said the sheep. "They are going to kill and eat you."

"Are they?" said the pig. "Well, I hope they'll say grace after meat."

"If you do as I do," said the sheep, "we'll go off to the wood, build us a house, and set up for ourselves. A home is a home be it ever so homely."

Yes! The pig was willing enough. "Good company is such a comfort," he said, and so the two set off.

So, when they had gone a bit they met a goose.

"Good day, good sirs, and thanks for our last merry meeting," said the goose. "Where are you going so fast today?"

'Good day, and the same to you," said the sheep. "You must know we were too well off at home, and so we are going to set up for ourselves in the wood, for you know every man's house is his castle."

"Well!" said the goose, "it's much the same with me where I am. Can't I go with you too, for it's child's play when three share the day."

"With gossip and gabble is built neither house nor stable," said the pig, "let us know what you can do."

"By cunning and skill a cripple can do what he will," said the goose. "I can pluck moss and stuff it into the seams of the planks, and your house will be tight and warm."

Yes! they would give him leave, for, above all things piggy wished to be warm and comfortable.

So, when they had gone a bit farther, the goose having hard work of it to walk so fast, they met a hare, who came frisking out of the wood.

"Good day, good sirs, and thanks for our last merry meeting," she said, "how far are you trotting today?"

"Good day, and the same to you," said the sheep. "We were far too well off at home, and so we're going to the wood, to build us a house, and set up for ourselves, for you know, try all the world round, there's nothing like home."

"As for that," said the hare, "I have a house in every bush, yes, a house in every bush, but, yet, I have often said, in winter, "'if I only live till summer, I'll build me a house,' and so I have half a mind to go with you and build one up, after all."

"Yes!" said the pig. "If we ever get into a scrape, we might use you to scare away the dogs, for you don't fancy you could help us in house building."

"He who lives long enough always finds work enough to do," said the hare. 'I have teeth to gnaw pegs, and paws to drive them into the wall, so I can very well set up to be a carpenter, for 'good tools make good work,' as the man said, when he flayed the mare with a gimlet."

Yes! she too got leave to go with them and build their house, there was nothing more to be said about it.

When they had gone a bit farther they met a cock.

"Good day, good sirs," said the cock, "and thanks for our last merry meeting. Where are you going today, gentlemen?'

"Good day, and the same to you," said the sheep. "At home we were too well off, and so we are going off to the wood to build us a house, and set up for ourselves, for he who out of doors shall bake, loses at last both coal and cake."

"Well!" said the cock, "that's just my case, but it's better to sit on one's own perch, for then one can never be left in the lurch, and, besides, all cocks crow loudest at home. Now, if I might have leave to join such a gallant company, I also would like to go to the wood and build a house."

"Ay! Ay!" said the pig, "flapping and crowing sets tongues a-going, but a jaw on a stick never yet laid a brick. How can you ever help us to build a house?"

"Oh!" said the cock, "that house will never have a clock, where there is neither dog nor cock. I am up early, and I wake everyone."

"Very true," said the pig, "the morning hour has a golden dower, so let him come with us, for, you must know, piggy is always the soundest sleeper. 'Sleep is the biggest thief,' he says, and he thinks nothing of stealing half one's life."

So they all set off to the wood, as a band and brotherhood, and built the house. The pig hewed the timber, and the sheep drew it home. The hare was carpenter, and gnawed pegs and bolts, and hammered them into the walls and roof. The goose plucked moss and stuffed it into the seams, while the cock crew, and looked out that they did not oversleep themselves in the morning, and when the house was ready, and the roof lined with birch bark, and thatched with turf, there they lived by themselves, and were merry and well.

"Tis good to travel east and west," said the sheep, "but after all a home is best."

But you must know that a bit farther on in the wood was a wolf's den, and there lived two greylegs. So when they saw that a new house had risen up nearby, they wanted to know what sort of folk their neighbours were, for they thought to themselves that a good neighbour was better than a brother in a foreign land, and that it was better to live in a good neighbourhood than to know many people miles and miles off.

So one of them made up an errand, and went into the new house and asked for a light for his pipe. But as soon as ever he got inside the door, the sheep gave him such a butt that he fell head foremost into the stove. Then the pig began to gore and bite him, the goose to nip and peck him, the cock upon the roost to crow and chatter, and as for the hare she was so frightened out of her wits, that she ran about aloft and on the floor, and scratched and scrambled in every corner of the house.

So after a long time the wolf came out.

"Well!" said the one who waited for him outside, "neighbourhood makes brotherhood. You must have come into a perfect paradise on bare earth, since you stayed so long. But what became of the light, for you have neither pipe nor smoke."

"Yes, yes!' said the other; "it was just a nice light and a pleasant company. Such manners I never saw in all my life. But then you know we can't pick and choose in this wicked world, and an unbidden guest gets bad treatment. As soon as I got inside the door, the shoe-maker let fly at me with his last, so that I fell head foremost into the stithy fire, and there sat two smiths who blew the bellows and made the sparks fly, and beat and punched me with red hot tongs and pincers, so that they tore whole pieces out of my body. As for the hunter he went scrambling about looking for his gun, and it was good luck he did not find it.

"And all the while there was another who sat up under the roof, and slapped his arms and sang out, 'Put a hook into him, and drag him here, drag him there.' That was what he screamed, and if he had only got hold of me, I should never have come out alive."

The Pig in the Dining-Room

An English Tale

This tale is my version of a story told by Andrew Lang in his book The Book Of Dreams And Ghosts, published by Longmans, Green And Co., London & New York, in 1899.

Although he's now celebrated for his Coloured Fairy Books (like The Blue Fairy Book, The Green Fairy Book, etc.), Lang himself wasn't the one actually collecting the tales. H—his wife, Leonora Blanche Alleyne Lang, did much of the translating, adapting, and editing. Lang was more the public face, while she quietly did the heavy lifting behind the scenes. What's odd is that for decades her contribution went almost entirely unacknowledged, even though without her, the "Andrew Lang Fairy Books" might not exist in the form we know them today.

Long ago, when the old Palace of Hereford was still filled with bishops and their families, there lived a lady named Mrs. Atlay, the Bishop's wife. She was a thoughtful woman, given to order and good sense, though in her heart she carried a touch of superstition, as many folk in England once did.

One night, as the bells tolled midnight across the quiet city, Mrs. Atlay dreamed a dream so strange it jolted her awake.

141

She thought she saw a pig, an ordinary farm pig, pink and coarse-haired, wandering about in the grand dining-room, rooting its snout against the carved oak panels as if searching for acorns.

When dawn came, she rose and went down the staircase, her gown sweeping along the cold stone steps. In the great hall she found her children gathered with their governess, waiting for morning prayers. With a little laugh, though half uneasy, she told them of her dream:

"Would you believe it? I saw a pig in the dining-room last night."

The governess chuckled. The children clapped their hands, delighted with the oddity of it. A pig belonged in the sty, or the muddy lane beyond the orchard, not in the palace where silver candlesticks gleamed and the long table was set with shining glass.

After prayers, the family still talking of the dream, Mrs. Atlay led them into the dining-room. She opened the heavy door, only to stop short.

There, in truth, stood a pig.

It was a plump fellow, streaked with mud from the sty, grunting contentedly as though it had every right to be there. It nosed about the carpet, leaving prints upon the floor that no brush would quite erase. The governess shrieked. The children squealed with laughter. And Mrs. Atlay, though a sensible woman, felt the hairs prickle on her neck, for she knew she had spoken of the beast before any soul had entered that room.

Later it was discovered that the pig had broken loose from its pen in the yard just after dawn. It had wandered through a side door carelessly left unlatched, and so found its way into the Bishop's palace as though summoned.

Now, folk will argue about such things. Some say it was nothing more than chance, a dream like any other, and a pig behaving as pigs do. Others say that dreams sometimes walk ahead of us, showing what the day will bring. And there are those who shake their heads and tell the tale only to make children laugh, as a warning that pigs and bishops make strange company.

But to this day, in Hereford, if you speak of the Atlay household, someone will remember the morning when a lady dreamed of a pig in the dining-room, and found it waiting for her, just as the dream foretold.

The Lion and the Boar

An Indian Tale

This tale is adapted from a story told by W.H.D. Rouse in his book The Giant Crab and Other Tales from Old India, published by David Nutt, London, in 1897.

W.H.D. Rouse (1863–1950) was a British classical scholar, translator, and folklorist best known for promoting the "Direct Method" of teaching Greek and Latin, encouraging students to learn the ancient languages by speaking and hearing them, rather than only through grammar drills. He served as headmaster of the Perse School in Cambridge and produced widely read prose translations of Homer, Apuleius, and other classical works. Alongside his classical scholarship, Rouse also collected and retold folktales from many cultures, publishing volumes such as Folk-Tales of All Nations (1914) and The Talking Thrush and Other Tales from India (1899).

Once upon a time there was a Lion who lived in the mountains, and he used to drink water out of a beautiful lake. It so happened that, as he was drinking there one day, he saw a Boar feeding over on the opposite bank. Now he had just eaten a leg of elephant, and was not hungry; but he made a note of that Boar, thinking to himself what a nice meal the Boar would make some other day. So, after drinking his fill, he crawled quietly away through the bushes, hoping that the Boar could not see him.

But the Boar had sharp eyes, and did see him. "Hello!" he said to himself, "that Lion is afraid of me, that's clear! Ah well, he shouldn't try to get away so easily. If he wants to go, he must fight me first!"

He puffed his chest out very big, and rubbed his tusks against a tree, then he called out:

"Stay, stay, runaway!

Let us have a fight today!

You have four feet, so have I!

If you fail, you can but try!"

The Lion could hardly believe his ears. What! A Boar challenge him to fight! He could break a Boar's back with a tap of his paw. Still, he hid his astonishment at this impertinent Boar and only said, "Please, Mr. Boar, let me off today, as I'm rather tired. I have just been wrestling with a fox. But, if you like, I will meet you here this day week, and then we can fight it out between us."

He said this so humbly that the Boar became haughtier than ever. "Oh, very well," he said, "it shall never be said I took advantage of anyone. This day week, then! Good-day to you."

145

When he got home, his friends hardly knew him. Every bristle on his back was standing up straight, and his little greedy eyes were gleaming. He ran into the house, knocking over the pots and pans, snarling at his wife, and making himself very disagreeable indeed. At last the other Boars protested, and said they would not stand it any longer.

"Oh!" said the boar, , "you defy a Boar that has killed a Lion! Come on, then!" and very fierce indeed he looked.

Killed a Lion! They all looked shocked. "Where is the Lion you have killed?" asked a pretty little sow, full of curiosity.

"Well, I haven't exactly killed him yet," said the Boar rather unwillingly. "He is coming to be killed this day week."

"What on earth do you mean?" his friends asked.

He told them the story, but he did not feel quite so bold now as he had felt before. And when he finished, he felt worse than ever, for one and all they set up such a weeping and wailing that the whole forest resounded with it! "Oh dear, oh dear!" they cried, "you'll be the death of us! Kill a Lion? Why, he will crunch you up in a trice, and then he'll come here, and we are all dead Boars!"

By this time the poor Boar had lost all his conceit. You see he was an ignorant Boar, and did not know at all what the strength of a Lion is. So his heart was down in his toes, and all he wanted now was some way out of the mischief. Nobody could think of a way, until one very old and wise Boar advised him to roll in the mud till he was very dirty, because Lions are clean beasts and do not like dirt.

So every day he rolled and wallowed in the dirtiest places he could find, and by the appointed time he was like a big cake of dirt. So when he came to the lake where he was to meet the Lion, the wind took a whiff of him to the Lion, and the Lion gave a jump, and snuffed, and sneezed, and swished his tail, and cried out, "Get to leeward, get to leeward! Here's a pretty trick! Well, you have saved your life. I wouldn't touch you with a pair of tongs now!" and, in great disgust he went away, saying, as he went, this little rhyme:

"Dirty Boar, I want no more,
You're saved from being eaten;
If you would fight, I yield me quite,
And own that I am beaten!"

You may be sure that our friend the Boar did not wait any longer, but scampered off home. But when he got there, I am sorry to say he told all his friends he had beaten the Lion, and the Lion had run away! He certainly had beaten the Lion in one way, but not in fair fight, so it was rather mean to pretend he had. However, nobody believed him, and the colony of Boars thought the best thing they could do was to get away from that place as fast as their four legs could carry them.

"If he is beaten," they said with a wink, "after all, he is still a Lion."

The Wild Boar and the Fox

A Traditional Fable

This tale is my own versions of a traditional fable taken from various sources in my own collection of folk and fairy tales.

The Wild Boar and the Fox is one of the many fables attributed to Aesop, the Greek fabulist of the 6th century BCE (though many of the stories were transmitted and reshaped by later collectors).

The tale appears in Latin collections of Aesop's fables during antiquity and the Middle Ages, especially in the versions preserved by Phaedrus (1st century CE, Rome) and later by Babrius (2nd century CE, in Greek verse).

From there, it entered the stock of medieval European fables, used in moralizing sermons and school texts.

One crisp autumn morning, deep in the forest, a wild boar stood before a tall oak tree. The ground was carpeted with golden leaves, and the air smelled of damp earth and mushrooms. The boar pressed his massive body close to the tree and began to grind his tusks against its bark, back and forth, back and forth, until sparks seemed almost to fly.

Nearby, a fox slunk out of the underbrush. His coat gleamed red in the sun, and his sharp eyes caught the strange sight of the boar polishing his tusks. The fox sat back on his haunches and smirked.

"Well now," said the fox, curling his tail around him. "That looks like hard work. Tell me, friend Boar, why waste your morning on such tiresome business? There are no hunters in sight, no dogs baying in the distance. Surely this is the season for sleeping late and rooting up acorns, not wearing your tusks down on tree-bark."

The boar paused, his tusks gleaming sharper than before. He turned his great head slowly and fixed the fox with one eye. "You speak lightly," said the boar, his voice as low as thunder, "because you are quick of foot and sly of tongue. When danger comes, you slip into a hole or dart into the brambles. But I am no fox. When danger comes for me, I must stand and fight."

The fox flicked his ears and laughed. "But there is no danger! Look around you. The woods are quiet. The hunters are still in their villages. The hounds are chained. Why trouble yourself with such grim thoughts when all is peaceful?"

The boar bent again to his task, tusks grating against the bark. His breath came in steady puffs, and his muscles rippled as he worked.

"You see no danger," he rumbled, "because danger is not here yet. But the wise beast prepares when the forest is quiet, so that when the dogs do come, and the horns sound, and the spears glitter through the trees, I will not waste my time sharpening tusks then. I will already be ready."

149

The fox opened his mouth to reply, but at that very moment, the sound of a horn echoed faintly across the hills. The fox's ears shot up. Dogs barked in the distance.

Without another word, the fox bolted into the brambles, his tail flashing as he disappeared.

The boar stood tall, his tusks honed and gleaming, and waited, for wisdom sharpens its tools before danger arrives. Only the fool waits until the fight is already upon him.

Peter-Of-The-Pigs

A Portuguese Tale

This tale is adapted from a story told by Elsie Spicer Eells in her book The Islands of Magic, published by Harcourt, Brace And Co., New York, in 1922.

Elsie Spicer Eells (1880–1963) was an American folklorist best known for collecting and publishing fairy tales and folk narratives from Latin America, particularly Brazil, as well as Spain and Portugal. She travelled widely, often working with oral storytellers, and recorded tales that blended Indigenous, African, and European traditions. Eells had a gift for retelling oral traditions in clear, literary English while preserving their local flavour, and her work helped bring the richness of Ibero-American and Brazilian folklore into the broader canon of world fairy tales during the early 20th century.

Long ago there lived a man who employed a boy to take care of his pigs. The lad's name was Peter and he was commonly called by everyone in the countryside Peter-of-the-pigs.

One day a man came up to him and said, "Sell me these seven pigs."

151

"I can't sell but six of them," said Peter. "I must keep one, but you may buy the other six if you will cut off their tails and ears and leave them for me."

The man promised to do this, and the boy pocketed the money. The six pigs looked sad enough without their tails and ears as they were driven away by their new master.

Peter led his one remaining pig down to the sand pit. He buried it halfway in the sand. He buried the tails and ears of the other six pigs, too, so that part of them stuck out. Then he ran with all speed for his master.

"Come and help me get the pigs out of the sand pit!" he called out.

His master ran as fast as he could to the sand pit. There he saw one of the pigs halfway out of the sand. He and Peter together soon pulled it out completely. Then he took hold of the tail nearby. To his horror it appeared to break off in his hand.

"Run to the house and ask my wife to give you two shovels!" cried the owner of the pigs. "With the shovels we can dig out the rest of the pigs."

The boy ran to the house. He knew that his master kept his money in two big bags.

"My master says that you shall give me his two money bags," said Peter to his mistress.

The woman did not approve of doing this. "Are you sure he said both of them?" she asked.

"Yes, both of them," said Peter. "Go ask him yourself."

Accordingly, the woman ran out of the house.

"Did you say both of them?" she called to her husband.

"Yes, both of them," he replied. "Be quick about it, too."

Of course the poor man thought that she was asking about the two shovels which he had sent Peter to get.

Thus Peter received his master's two bags of money, and set out into the world with the bags on his shoulder and his pockets full of the money he had obtained from the sale of the six pigs.

After a time Peter-of-the-pigs met a robber. The robber stole one of his money bags and ran away with it. Peter ran after him.

Now it happened that the robber had just killed a deer. He was carrying the liver inside his blouse. As he ran he threw it back so that he could run faster, and Peter saw what he had done.

"If you want to catch me, you'll have to throw away your liver, too," called out the robber over his shoulder.

Peter-of-the-pigs pulled out his knife and cut out his liver. Of course he dropped dead at once.

When at last Peter's master found out that he had been deceived he ran after the lad. As he found him lying dead there by the wayside, he said, "Oh, Peter-of-the-pigs! You were sharp, but you found someone who was sharper."

Thus it is in life.

This Is The Lad Who Sold The Pig

A Norwegian Tale

This tale is adapted from a story told by Peter Christen Asbjørnsen in his book Tales from the Fjeld, published by Chapman & Hall, London, in 1874.

Oddly, the fairy-tale collector was also a fish-oil technologist. In the 1850s–60s Peter Christen Asbjørnsen ran government investigations into cod-liver oil production, performed chemical / heat-processing experiments to deodorise and clarify the oil, and published a technical treatise that helped upgrade Norway's export quality. So the man who gave us The Three Billy Goats Gruff also tinkered with vats, condensers, and temperature curves, making children's literature by day and better fish oil by night.

Once on a time there was a widow who had a son and he had set his heart on being nothing else than a tradesman. But you must know they were so poor that they had nothing that he could begin his trading with. The only thing his mother owned in the world was a sow pig, and he begged and prayed so long and so prettily for it, that at last she was forced to let him have it.

"When he got the sow he set off to sell it, so that he might have some money to begin his trading. So he offered it to this man and that, good and bad alike, but there was no one who just then cared to buy a pig. At last he came to a rich old hunks, but you know much will always have more, and that man was one of the sort that never can have enough.

"Will you buy a pig to-day?" said the lad, "a good pig, and a long pig, and a fine fat pig." That was what he said.

The old hunks asked what he would have for it. It was at least worth six dollars, even between brothers, said the lad, but the times were hard, and money so scarce that he didn't mind selling it for four dollars. And that was as good as giving it away.

No, that the old hunks would not do. In fact he wouldn't give so much as a dollar even, for he had more pigs already than he wanted, and was well off for pigs of that sort. But as the lad was so eager to sell, he would be willing to do him a turn, and deal with him, but the most he could give for the whole pig, every inch of it, was fourpence. If he would take that down, he might turn his pig into the sty with the rest. That was what the old hunks said.

The lad thought it shameful that he should not get more for his pig, but then he thought that something was better than nothing, and so he took the fourpence and turned in the pig. And then he counted the money and went about his business. But when he got out into the road, he could not get it out of his head that he had been cheated out of his pig, and that he was not much better off with fourpence than with nothing. The longer he went and thought of this the angrier he got, and at last he thought to himself, "If I could only play him a pretty trick, I wouldn't care either for the pig or the pence."

So he went away and got a pair of stout thongs and a cat-o'-nine-tails, and then he threw on a big cloak, and put on a billy goat's beard, and so he went back to the skinflint and said he was from outlandish parts, where he had learnt to be a master builder, for you must know he had already heard that the old hunks was going to build a house.

Yes, he would gladly take him as master builder, the old hunks said, for thereabouts there were none but home-taught carpenters. So off they went to look at the timber, and it was the finest heart of pine that anyone would wish to have in the wall of his house, and even the lad said it was brave timber, for he couldn't say otherwise, but, he commented, in outlandish parts they had a new fashion, which was far better than the old. They did not take long beams and fit them into the wall. Instead they cut the beams up into nice small logs, and then they baked them in the sun and fastened them together again, and so they wore both stronger and prettier than an old-fashioned timber building.

"That's how they build all the houses now-a-days in outlandish parts," said the lad.

"If it must be so, it must," said the hunks. With that he set all the carpenters and woodmen who were to be found round about to chop and hew all his beams up into small logs.

"But," said the lad, "we still want some big trees, some of the real mast-firs, for our sill-beams. Maybe, there are no such big trees in your wood?"

"Well!" said the man, "if they're not to be found in my wood, it will be hard to find them anywhere else."

And so they strode off to the wood, both of them, and a little way up the hill they came to a big tree.

"I should think that's big enough," said the man.

"No, it isn't big enough," said the lad. "If you haven't bigger trees, we shan't make much way with our building after the new fashion."

"Yes! I have bigger ones," said the man. "You shall soon see, but we must go further on."

So they went a long way over the hill, and at last they came to a big tree, one of the finest trees for a mast in all the wood.

"Do you think this is big enough?" said the man.

"I almost think it is," said the lad. "We will fathom it, and then we shall soon see. You go on the other side of the fir, and I will stand here. If we are not good enough to make our hands meet, it will be big enough, but mind you stretch out well. Stretch out well, do you hear?" said the lad, as he took out his thongs. As for the man, he did all that the lad told him to do.

"Yes!" said the lad, "we shall meet nicely, I can see. But stop a bit, and I'll stretch your hands better," he said, as he slipped a running knot over the man's wrists and drew it tight and bound him fast to the tree. Then out came the cat-o'-nine-tails, and he fell to flogging the old hunks as fast as he could, and all the while he cried out, "'This is the lad who sold the pig, and this is the lad who sold the pig.'

157

Nor did he leave off till he thought the old hunks had enough, and that he had got his rights for the pig, and then he loosed him, and left him lying under the tree.

Now when the man did not come home they made a hue and cry for him over the neighbourhood, and searched the country round, and at last they found him under the fir-tree, more dead than alive.

So when they had got him home the lad came, and had dressed himself up as a doctor, and said he had come from foreign parts, and knew a cure for all kinds of hurt. And when the man heard that, he was all for having him to doctor him, and the lad said he would not be long in curing him, but he must have him all alone in a room by himself, and no one must be by.

"If you hear him screech and cry out," he said, "you must not mind it, for the more he screeches, the sooner he will be well again."

So when they were alone, he said, "First of all I must bleed you."

And so he threw the man roughly down on a bench and bound him fast with the thongs, and then out came the cat-o'-nine-tails, and he fell to flogging him as fast as he could. The man screeched and screamed, for his back was sore, and every lash went into the bare flesh, and the lad flogged and flogged as though there were no end to it and all the while he bawled out, "'This is the lad who sold the pig. This is the lad who sold the pig.'

The old hunks bellowed as though a knife were being stuck into him, but there was not a soul that cared about it, for the more he screeched the sooner he would be well, they thought.

So when the lad had done his doctoring, he set off from the farm as fast as he could, but they followed fast on his heels, and overtook him and threw him into prison, and the end was he was doomed to be hanged.

And the old hunks was so angry with him, even then, that he would not have him hanged till he was quite well, so that he might hang him with his own hands.

While the lad sat there in prison waiting to be hanged, one of the serving-men came out by night and stole kail in the garden of the old hunks, and the lad saw him.

"So, so!" said he to himself. "Master thief, it will be odd if I don't play off a trick or two with you before I am hanged."

And so when time went on, and the man was so well he thought he had strength enough to hang the lad, he made them set up a gallows down by the way to the mill, so that he might see the body hanging every time he went to the mill. So they set out to hang the lad, and when they had gone a bit of the way, the lad said, "You will not refuse to let me talk alone with your servant who grinds down yonder at the mill? I did him a bad turn once, and I wish now to confess it, and beg him for forgiveness before I die."

Yes, he might have leave to do that.

"Heaven help you!" he said to the miller's man. "Now your master is coming to hang you because you stole kail in his garden."

As soon as the miller's man heard that, he was so taken aback he did not know which way to turn, and so he asked the lad what he should do.

"Take and change clothes with me and hide yourself behind the door," said the lad; "and then he will not know who is who, and if he lays hands on anyone, then it will not be you, but me."

It was some time before they had changed clothes and dressed again, and the old hunks began to be afraid lest the lad should have run away. So he went down to the mill door.

"Where is he?" he said to the lad, who stood there as white as a miller.

"Oh, he was here just now," said the lad. "I think he went and hid himself behind the door."

"I'll teach you to hide behind the door, you rogue," said the old hunks, as he seized the man in a great rage, and hurried him off to the gallows and hanged him in a breath, and all the while he never knew it was not the lad that he hanged.

After that was done, he wanted to go into the mill to talk to his man, who was busy grinding. Meantime the lad had wedged up the upper millstone, and was feeling under it with his hands.

Come here, come here," he called out as soon as he saw the old hunks, "and you shall feel what a wonderful millstone this is."

So the man went and felt the millstone with one hand.

"Nay, nay," said the lad, "'you'll never feel it unless you take hold of it with both hands."

Well, he did so, and just then the lad snatched out the wedge and let the upper millstone down on him, so that he was caught fast by the hands between the stones. Then out came the cat-o'-nine-tails again, and he fell to flogging him as fast as he could.

"This is the lad who sold the pig," he cried out, till he was hoarse.

And when he had flogged him as much as he could he went home to his mother, and as time went on, and he thought the old hunks might have come to himself again, he said to her, "Now I daresay that man to whom I sold the pig will be coming, and now I know no other trick to screen me any longer from him, unless I dig a hole here south of the house, and there I will lie all day, and you must mind and say to him just what I tell you.'

So the lad told his mother all she was to say and do.

Then he dug a hole, and took with him a long butcher's knife, and he lay down in it, and his mother covered him over with boughs, and leaves, and moss, so that he was quite hidden. There he lay by day, and after a while the man came travelling along and asked for the lad.

"Ay, ay," said his mother. "He was a man, that he was, though he never got from me more than one sow pig. For he became both a doctor and a master builder, and he was hanged after that, and rose again from the dead, and yet I never heard anything but ill of him. Here he came flying home the other day, and then he gave me the greatest joy I ever had of him, for he laid down and died. As for me, I did not care enough for him to spend money on a priest and

Christian earth, so I just buried him there, south of the house, and raked over him some rotten boughs and leaves.'

"See now," said the old hunks, "if he hasn't cheated me after all, and slipped through my fingers. But though I have not been avenged on him living, I will do him a dishonour in his grave."

As he said this he strode away south to the grave, and stooped down to spit into it, but at that very moment the lad stuck the knife into him up to the handle, and bawled out, "'This is the lad who sold the pig! This is the lad who sold the pig!"

Away flew the man with the knife sticking in him, and he was so scared and afraid, that nothing has ever been heard or seen of him since.

A Dreadful Boar

A Chinese Tale

This tale is adapted from a story written by Adele M. Fielde and collected by Willam Patten in his book The Junior Classics, Volume 1, published by P. F. Collier & Son, New York, in 1912.

William Patten, an American naturalist and zoologist, and Adele M. Fielde, a missionary, linguist, and ethnographer, collaborated on collecting and publishing Chinese folk tales in the late 19th and early 20th centuries. Their work, presented traditional Chinese stories to Western audiences, blending Fielde's deep knowledge of Chinese language and culture with Patten's literary shaping for English readers. The collaboration preserved moral tales, fables, and wonder-stories from southern China, helping introduce Chinese oral traditions to the folklore scholarship and popular readership of the English-speaking world.

A poor old woman, who lived with her one little granddaughter in a wood, was out gathering sticks for fuel and found a green stalk of sugar-cane which she added to her bundle. She presently met an elf in the form of a Wild Boar, that asked her for the cane. She declined giving it to him, saying that at her age to stoop and to rise again was to earn what she picked up, and she was going to take the cane home and let her little granddaughter suck its sap.

The Boar, angry at her refusal, said that during the coming night he would come and eat her granddaughter instead of the cane, and went off into the wood.

When the old woman reached her cabin she sat down by the door and wailed, for she knew that she had no means of defending herself against the Boar. While she sat crying a vender of needles came along and asked her what the matter was. She told him, but all that he could do for her was to give her a box of needles. The Old Woman stuck the needles thickly over the lower half of the door, on its outer side, and then went on crying.

Just then a Man came along with a basket of crabs, heard her lamentations, and stopped to inquire what was the matter. She told him, but he said he knew of no help for her, but he would do the best he could for her by giving her half his crabs. The woman put the crabs in her water jar, behind her door, and again sat down and cried.

A Farmer, who was coming along from the fields, leading his ox, also asked the cause of her distress and heard her story. He said he was sorry that he could not think of any way of preventing the evil she expected, but that he would leave his ox to stay all night with her, as it might be a sort of company for her in her loneliness. She led the ox into her cabin, tied it to the head of her bedstead, gave it some straw, and then sat down to cry again.

A courier returning on horseback from a neighboring town was the next to pass her door, and he dismounted to inquire what troubled her. Having heard her tale, he said he would leave his horse to stay with her, and make the ox more contented. So she tied the horse to the foot of the bed, and, thinking how surely evil was coming upon her, she burst out crying anew.

A boy just then came along with a snapping turtle that he had caught and stopped to ask what had happened to her. On learning the cause of her weeping he said it was no use to contend against sprites, but that he would give her his snapping turtle as a proof of his sympathy. She took the turtle, tied it in front of her bedstead, and continued to cry.

Some men who were carrying millstones then came along, inquired into her trouble, and expressed their compassion by giving her a millstone, which they rolled into her back yard.

While they were doing this a Man went by carrying hoes and a pickaxe, and he stopped and asked her why she was crying so hard. She told him her grief, and he said he would gladly help her if he could, but he was only a well digger and could do nothing for her except to dig a well. She pointed out a place in the backyard, and he went to work and quickly dug a well.

On his departure the old woman cried again, until a Paper Seller came and inquired what the matter was. When she told him he gave her a large sheet of white paper, as a token of pity, and she laid it smoothly over the mouth of the well.

Nightfall came. The old woman shut and barred her door, put her granddaughter snugly on the wall side of the bed, and then lay down beside her to await the foe.

At midnight the Boar came and threw himself against the door to break it in. The needles wounded him sorely, so that when he had gained an entrance he was heated and thirsty, and went to the water jar to drink.

When he thrust in his snout the crabs attacked him, clung to his bristles, and pinched his ears, till he rolled over and over to free himself.

Then in a rage he approached the front of the bed; but the snapping turtle nipped his tail and made him retreat under the feet of the horse, who kicked him over to the ox, and the ox tossed him back to the horse. Thus beset, he was glad to escape to the back yard to take a rest and to consider the situation.

Seeing a clean paper spread on the ground, he went to lie upon it, and fell into the well. The Old Woman, hearing the fall, rushed out and rolled the millstone down on him and crushed him.

The Swine and the Sheep

A Traditional Fable

This tale is my own versions of a traditional fable taken from various sources in my own collection of folk and fairy tales. It is a variant of the tale, The Pigs In The Meadow, told later in this book. The Swine and the Sheep comes from the tradition of Aesop's Fables, originating in ancient Greece (c. 6th century BCE). It appears in the classical corpus of fables attributed to Aesop, though, like many of the fables, it was almost certainly passed down orally for centuries before being written down in Greek and later Latin.

There was once a quiet little farm where the days passed in rhythm with the seasons. The sheep lived contentedly in their pasture, cropping the grass and growing fat with fleece, while the pigs wallowed in the mud, snuffling for roots and scraps.

The sheep thought themselves noble creatures, mild and patient. The pigs, on the other hand, were noisy and rough, forever squealing at feeding time or squabbling.

The sheep often shook their heads and said, "What vulgar animals! Can they not keep silent for a moment?"

One afternoon, the shepherd entered the yard with his crook in hand. He walked past the sheep, who barely lifted their heads, and made his way straight to the pigpen. The pigs, sensing trouble, huddled together uneasily. Then the shepherd reached in and seized one plump young pig by the legs.

The pig erupted into a squeal so piercing that the air seemed to split. He kicked and writhed, his cries echoing across the hills. "Help! Help! He's killing me! He's taking me away!"

The whole farmyard stirred. Chickens flapped in fright, dogs barked, and even the cows turned their heads. The sheep, however, were irritated more than alarmed.

"Honestly," bleated one ewe, "what a fuss over nothing. We are handled by the shepherd all the time, and you don't hear us screaming like that."

"Yes," agreed another. "He takes us, shears us, and we stand calmly. No noise, no protest. Why must you carry on so?"

At that, the pig twisted his snout toward them and squealed all the louder. "You silly creatures! When he lays hands on you, it is only to take your wool. You lose a little coat and go free again, safe and sound. But when he carries me off, it is not for fleece, it is for flesh! He means to roast me for supper! Would you not scream then?"

The sheep fell silent. They looked at one another and understood, at last, the reason for the pig's terrible cries. None of them mocked him again, for now they understood that it is easy to condemn another's cries until you know the weight of their suffering.

The Camel and the Pig

An Indian Tale

This tale is my version of a brief story told by Ramaswami Raju and collected by Willam Patten in his book The Junior Classics, Volume 1, published by P. F. Collier & Son, New York, in 1912.

Ramaswami Raju and William Patten both worked at the turn of the 20th century to make non-European folklore accessible to English-speaking readers, though from very different vantage points. Raju, a South Indian writer, gathered and retold Indian animal fables and moral tales in English, often blending the didactic tone of Panchatantra-style stories with a modern literary polish, helping preserve Indian oral traditions during a time of colonial transition.

In the days when beasts still argued as men do, there lived a Camel and a Pig who were neighbours. They were forever quarrelling, for each thought his own shape the better, and neither would yield to the other.

One morning, as the sun rose red over the village fields, the Camel lifted his great head above the acacia trees and said with pride, "Ah, Pig! There is nothing in the world like being tall. Look at me, my head brushes the very clouds! Wherever

169

there are leaves, I may reach them. Wherever there are branches, I may taste them. What creature is blessed like I am?"

The Pig, who was wallowing happily in a cool puddle at the roadside, snorted and said, "Pooh! Tall? What use is tall? Nothing like being short, I tell you. Look at me, I can go where I please. I creep under fences, I slip through hedges, and I have no need to strain my neck. Shortness is the true blessing."

The Camel rumbled in his throat and said, "Well then! If I cannot prove the worth of my tallness, I shall give up my hump."

The Pig squealed, "And if I cannot prove the worth of my shortness, I shall give up my snout."

"Agreed!" said the Camel, shaking his long neck.

"Agreed!" said the Pig, twitching his muddy nose.

And off they went together to test their fortunes.

Not far from the village, they came upon a garden surrounded by a low mud wall. There was no gate and no opening, only the wall standing between them and the lush greenery inside. The Pig leapt at the wall, but it was too high for him to see beyond. He trotted back and forth, snuffling in vain. But the Camel stretched his neck, reached easily over, and pulled down handfuls of beans and fresh gourds, chewing them with delight.

With his mouth full, the Camel looked down at the Pig and said mockingly, "Now, friend Pig, would you rather be tall or short?"

The Pig grumbled but said nothing. They walked on.

Soon they reached another garden, and this one was different. It was surrounded by a high stone wall, so high that even the Camel's head could not peer over it. But at one end there was a little wicket gate, so low and narrow that only a small beast could pass.

The Camel bent and pushed, but his great body could not squeeze through. The Pig, however, darted inside with ease. He found rows of vegetables, roots, and melons, and ate until his sides were round. Then he trotted back out through the gate, licking his snout and laughing.

"Now, friend Camel," he said, "would you rather be tall or short?"

The Camel sighed, and the Pig grunted, and together they thought the matter over. At last they said, "Let the Camel keep his hump and the Pig his snout. Tall is good where tall will do, and short is good in its place too. Every creature is made as he is meant to be."

And so they ceased their quarrel, though it is said that, even now, Camels carry pride in their necks and Pigs in their noses.

Story of the Holy Boar

An Indian Tale

This tale is adapted from a story told by Somadeva Bhatta in his book The Kathá Sarit Ságara, translated by C. H. Tawney and published by the Baptist Mission Press in 1884.

Somadeva Bhatta was an 11th-century Kashmiri poet and folklorist, best known for compiling the Kathá Sarit Ságara ("Ocean of the Streams of Story"), one of the largest collections of Indian tales ever written. Drawing on an even older lost work, the Bṛhatkathā, he wove together hundreds of folktales, fables, romances, and adventure stories into an immense Sanskrit narrative framed around the adventures of Prince Naraváhanadatta. His work is fascinating not only because it preserves ancient Indian oral traditions, but also because it became a bridge across cultures. Many of its tales travelled westward through translations, influencing Arabic, Persian, and even European folklore.

Long ago there dwelt in a cavern in the Vindhya mountains a wise boar, who was an incarnation of a portion of a Buddha. He lived, together with his friend, a monkey. He was a benefactor of all creatures, and he always stayed in the society of that friend, honouring guests, and so he spent his

172

time in occupations suited to him. But once on a time there came a storm lasting for five days, which was terrible, in that it hindered with its constant rainfall the movements of all living creatures. On the fifth day, as the boar was lying asleep with the monkey, a lion came to the door of the cave with his mate and his cub.

Then the lion said to his mate, "During this long period of bad weather we shall certainly die of hunger from not obtaining any animal to eat."

The lioness answered, "It is clear that hunger will prevent all of us from surviving, so you two had better eat me and so save your lives. For you are my lord and master, and this son of ours is our very life. You will easily get another mate like me, so ensure the welfare of you two by devouring me."

Now, as chance would have it, that noble boar woke up and heard the conversation of the lion and his mate. And he was delighted, and thought to himself, "The idea of my receiving such guests on such a night in such a storm! Ah! Today my merit in a former state of existence has brought forth fruit. So let me satiate these guests with this body that perishes in a moment, while I have a chance of doing so."

Having thus reflected, the boar rose up, and went out, and said to the lion with an affectionate voice, "My good friend, do not despair, for here I am ready to be eaten by you and your mate and your cub, so eat me."

When the boar said this, the lion was delighted and said to his mate, "Let this cub eat first, then I will eat, and you shall eat after me."

She agreed, and first the cub ate some of the flesh of the boar, and then the lion himself began to eat. And while he was eating, the noble boar said to him, "Drink my blood quickly, before it sinks into the ground, and satisfy your hunger with my flesh, and let your mate eat the rest."

While the boar was saying this, the lion gradually devoured his flesh until nothing but bones was left, but still the virtuous boar did not die, for his life remained in him. Meanwhile the lioness, exhausted with hunger, died in the cave, and the lion went off somewhere or other with his cub, and the night came to an end.

At this juncture his friend the monkey woke up, and went out, and seeing the boar reduced to such a condition, said to him in the utmost excitement, "Who reduced you to such a state? Tell me, my friend, if you can."

Thereupon the heroic boar told him the whole story. Then the monkey prostrated himself at his feet, and said to him with tears, "You must be a portion of some divinity, since you have thus rescued yourself from this animal nature, so tell me any wish that you may have, and I will endeavour to fulfil it for you."

When the monkey said this to the boar, the boar answered, "Friend, the only wish that I have is one difficult for even Destiny to fulfil. For my heart longs that I may recover my body as before, and that this unfortunate lioness that died of hunger before my eyes, may return to life, and satiate her hunger by devouring me."

While the boar was saying this, the God of Justice appeared in bodily form, and stroking him with his hand, turned him into a chief of sages possessing a celestial body. And he said to him, "It was I that assumed the form of this lion, and lioness, and cub, and produced this whole illusion, because I wished to conquer you who are exclusively intent on benefiting your fellow-creatures. But you, possessing perfect goodness, gave your life for others, and so have triumphed over me the God of Justice, and gained this rank of a chief of sages."

The sage, hearing this, and seeing the God of Justice standing in front of him, said, "Holy lord, this rank of chief of sages, even though attained, gives me no pleasure, since my friend this monkey has not as yet thrown off his animal nature."

When the god of Justice heard this, he turned the monkey also into a sage. Then the god of Justice and the dead lioness disappeared.

The Enchanted Pig

A Rumanian Tale

This tale is adapted from a story told by Andrew Lang in his book The Red Fairy Book, published by Longmans, Green And Co., London & New York, in 1890.

Although he's now celebrated for his Coloured Fairy Books (like The Blue Fairy Book, The Green Fairy Book, etc.), Lang himself wasn't the one actually collecting the tales, his wife, Leonora Blanche Alleyne Lang, did much of the translating, adapting, and editing. Lang was more the public face, while she quietly did the heavy lifting behind the scenes. What's odd is that for decades her contribution went almost entirely unacknowledged, even though without her, the "Andrew Lang Fairy Books" might not exist in the form we know them today.

Once upon a time there lived a King who had three daughters. Now it happened that he had to go out to battle, so he called his daughters and said to them, "My dear children, I am obliged to go to the wars. The enemy is approaching us with a large army. It is a great grief to me to leave you all. During my absence take care of yourselves and be good girls, behave well and look after everything in the house. You may walk in the garden, and you may go into all the rooms in the palace, except the room at the back in the right-hand corner. Into that you must not enter, for harm will befall you."

"You may keep your mind easy, father," they replied. "We have never been disobedient to you. Go in peace, and may heaven give you a glorious victory!"

When everything was ready for his departure, the King gave them the keys of all the rooms and reminded them once more of what he had said. His daughters kissed his hands with tears in their eyes, and wished him prosperity, and he gave the eldest the keys.

Now when the girls found themselves alone they felt so sad and dull that they did not know what to do. So, to pass the time, they decided to work for part of the day, to read for part of the day, and to enjoy themselves in the garden for part of the day. As long as they did this all went well with them. But this happy state of things did not last long. Every day they grew more and more curious, and you will see what the end of that was.

"Sisters," said the eldest Princess, "all day long we sew, spin, and read. We have been several days quite alone, and there is no corner of the garden that we have not explored. We have been in all the rooms of our father's palace, and have admired the rich and beautiful furniture. Why should not we go into the room that our father forbad us to enter?"

"Sister," said the youngest, "I cannot think how you can tempt us to break our father's command. When he told us not to go into that room he must have known what he was saying, and have had a good reason for saying it."

177

"Surely the sky won't fall about our heads if we do go in," said the second Princess. "Dragons and such like monsters that would devour us will not be hidden in the room. And how will our father ever find out that we have gone in?"

While they were speaking thus, encouraging each other, they had reached the room, and the eldest fitted the key into the lock, and snap, the door stood open.

The three girls entered, and what do you think they saw?

The room was quite empty, and without any ornament, but in the middle stood a large table, with a gorgeous cloth, and on it lay a big open book.

Now the Princesses were curious to know what was written in the book, especially the eldest, and this is what she read: "The eldest daughter of this King will marry a prince from the East."

Then the second girl stepped forward, and turning over the page she read: "The second daughter of this King will marry a prince from the West."

The girls were delighted, and laughed and teased each other.

But the youngest Princess did not want to go near the table or to open the book. Her elder sisters however left her no peace, and will she, nill she, they dragged her up to the table, and in fear and trembling she turned over the page and read: "The youngest daughter of this King will be married to a pig from the North."

Now if a thunderbolt had fallen upon her from heaven it would not have frightened her more. She almost died of misery, and if her sisters had not held her up, she would have sunk to the ground and cut her head open.

When she came out of the fainting fit into which she had fallen in her terror, her sisters tried to comfort her, saying, "How can you believe such nonsense? When did it ever happen that a king's daughter married a pig?"

"What a baby you are!" said the other sister. "Has not our father enough soldiers to protect you, even if the disgusting creature did come to woo you?"

The youngest Princess would love to have let herself be convinced by her sisters' words, and have believed what they said, but her heart was heavy. Her thoughts kept turning to the book, in which stood written that great happiness waited her sisters, but that a fate was in store for her such as had never before been known in the world.

Besides, the thought weighed on her heart that she had been guilty of disobeying her father. She began to get quite ill, and in a few days she was so changed that it was difficult to recognise her. Formerly she had been rosy and merry, now she was pale and nothing gave her any pleasure. She gave up playing with her sisters in the garden, ceased to gather flowers to put in her hair, and never sang when they sat together at their spinning and sewing.

In the meantime the King won a great victory, and having completely defeated and driven off the enemy, he hurried home to his daughters, to whom his thoughts had constantly turned. Everyone went out to meet him with cymbals and fifes and drums, and there was great rejoicing over his victorious return. The King's first act on reaching home was to thank Heaven for the victory he had gained over the enemies who had risen against him. He then entered his palace, and the three Princesses stepped forward to meet him. His joy was great when he saw that they were all well, for the youngest did her best not to appear sad.

In spite of this, however, it was not long before the King noticed that his third daughter was getting very thin and sad-looking. And all of a sudden he felt as if a hot iron were entering his soul, for it flashed through his mind that she had disobeyed his word. He felt sure he was right, but to be quite certain he called his daughters to him, questioned them, and ordered them to speak the truth. They confessed everything, but took good care not to say which had led the other two into temptation.

The King was so distressed when he heard it that he was almost overcome by grief. But he took heart and tried to comfort his daughters, who looked frightened to death. He saw that what had happened had happened, and that a thousand words would not alter matters by a hair's breadth.

Well, these events had almost been forgotten when one fine day a prince from the East appeared at the Court and asked the King for the hand of his eldest daughter. The King gladly gave his consent. A great wedding banquet was prepared, and after three days of feasting the happy pair were accompanied to the frontier with much ceremony and rejoicing.

After some time the same thing befell the second daughter, who was wooed and won by a prince from the West.

Now when the young Princess saw that everything fell out exactly as had been written in the book, she grew very sad.

180

She refused to eat, and would not put on her fine clothes nor go out walking, and declared that she would rather die than become a laughing-stock to the world. But the King would not allow her to do anything so wrong, and he comforted her in all possible ways.

So the time passed, till one fine day an enormous pig from the North walked into the palace, and going straight up to the King said, "Hail, oh King. May your life be as prosperous and bright as sunrise on a clear day!"

"I am glad to see you well, friend," answered the King, "but what wind has brought you here?"

"I come a-wooing," replied the Pig.

Now the King was astonished to hear so fine a speech from a Pig, and at once it occurred to him that something strange was the matter. He would gladly have turned the Pig's thoughts in another direction, as he did not wish to give him the Princess for a wife, but when he heard that the Court and the whole street were full of all the pigs in the world he saw that there was no escape, and that he must give his consent. The Pig was not satisfied with mere promises, but insisted that the wedding should take place within a week, and would not go away till the King had sworn a royal oath upon it.

The King then sent for his daughter, and advised her to submit to fate, as there was nothing else to be done. And he added, "My child, the words and whole behaviour of this Pig are quite unlike those of other pigs. I do not myself believe that he always was a pig. Depend upon it some magic or witchcraft has been at work. Obey him, and do everything that he wishes, and I feel sure that Heaven will shortly send you release."

"If you wish me to do this, dear father, I will do it," replied the girl.

In the meantime the wedding-day drew near. After the marriage, the Pig and his bride set out for his home in one of the royal carriages. On the way they passed a great bog, and the Pig ordered the carriage to stop, and got out and rolled about in the mire till he was covered with mud from head to foot. Then he got back into the carriage and told his wife to kiss him. What was the poor girl to do? She thought of her father's words, and, pulling out her pocket handkerchief, she gently wiped the Pig's snout and kissed it.

By the time they reached the Pig's dwelling, which stood in a thick wood, it was quite dark. They sat down quietly for a little, as they were tired after their drive, and then they had supper together, and lay down to rest. During the night the Princess noticed that the Pig had changed into a man. She was very surprised, but remembering her father's words, she took courage, determined to wait and see what would happen.

And now she noticed that every night the Pig became a man, and every morning he was changed into a Pig before she awoke. This happened several nights running, and the Princess could not understand it at all. Clearly her husband must be bewitched. In time she grew quite fond of him, for he was so kind and gentle.

One fine day as she was sitting alone she saw an old witch go past. She felt quite excited, as it was so long since she had seen a human being, and she called out to the old woman to come and talk to her. Among other things the witch told her that she understood all magic arts, and that she could foretell the future, and knew the healing powers of herbs and plants.

"I shall be grateful to you all my life, old dame," said the Princess, "if you will tell me what the matter with my husband is. Why is he a Pig by day and a human being by night?"

"I was just going to tell you that one thing, my dear, to show you what a good fortune-teller I am. If you like, I will give you a herb to break the spell."

"If you will only give it to me," said the Princess, "I will give you anything you choose to ask for, for I cannot bear to see him in this state."

"Here, then, my dear child," said the witch, "take this thread, but do not let him know about it, for if he did it would lose its healing power. At night, when he is asleep, you must get up very quietly, and fasten the thread round his left foot as firmly as possible; and you will see in the morning he will not have changed back into a Pig, but will still be a man. I do not want any reward. I shall be sufficiently repaid by knowing that you are happy. It almost breaks my heart to think of all you have suffered, and I only wish I had known it sooner, as I should have come to your rescue at once."

When the old witch had gone away the Princess hid the thread very carefully, and at night she got up quietly, and with a beating heart she bound the thread round her husband's foot. Just as she was pulling the knot tight there was a crack, and the thread broke, for it was rotten.

Her husband awoke with a start, and said to her, "Unhappy woman, what have you done? Three days more and this unholy spell would have fallen from me, and now, who knows how long I may have to go about in this disgusting shape? I must leave you at once, and we shall not meet again until you have worn out three pairs of iron shoes and blunted a steel staff in your search for me." So saying he disappeared.

Now, when the Princess was left alone she began to weep and moan in a way that was pitiful to hear, but when she saw that her tears and groans did her no good, she got up, determined to go wherever fate should lead her.

On reaching a town, the first thing she did was to order three pairs of iron sandals and a steel staff, and having made these preparations for her journey, she set out in search of her husband. On and on she wandered over nine seas and across nine continents, through forests with trees whose stems were as thick as beer-barrels, stumbling and knocking herself against the fallen branches, then picking herself up and going on. The boughs of the trees hit her face, and the shrubs tore her hands, but on she went, and never looked back. At last, wearied with her long journey and worn out and overcome with sorrow, but still with hope at her heart, she reached a house.

Now who do you think lived there? The Moon.

The Princess knocked at the door, and begged to be let in so that she might rest a little. The mother of the Moon, when she saw her sad plight, felt a great pity for her, and took her in and nursed and tended her. And while she was here the Princess had a little baby.

One day the mother of the Moon asked her, "How was it possible for you, a mortal, to get here to the house of the Moon?"

Then the poor Princess told her all that happened to her, and added "I shall always be thankful to Heaven for leading me here, and grateful to you that you took pity on me and on my baby, and did not leave us to die. Now I beg one last favour of you, can your daughter, the Moon, tell me where my husband is?"

"She cannot tell you that, my child," replied the goddess, "but, if you travel towards the East until you reach the dwelling of the Sun, he may be able to tell you something."

Then she gave the Princess a roast chicken to eat, and warned her to be very careful not to lose any of the bones, because they might be of great use to her.

When the Princess had thanked her once more for her hospitality and for her good advice, and had thrown away one pair of shoes that were worn out, and had put on a second pair, she tied up the chicken bones in a bundle, and taking her baby in her arms and her staff in her hand, she set out once more on her wanderings.

On and on and on she went across bare sandy deserts, where the roads were so heavy that for every two steps that she took forwards she fell back one, but she struggled on till she had passed these dreary plains. Next she crossed high rocky mountains, jumping from crag to crag and from peak to peak. Sometimes she would rest for a little on a mountain, and then start afresh always farther and farther on. She had to cross swamps and to scale mountain peaks covered with flints, so that her feet and knees and elbows were all torn and bleeding, and sometimes she came to a precipice across which she could not jump, and she had to crawl round on hands and knees, helping herself along with her staff.

At length, wearied to death, she reached the palace in which the Sun lived. She knocked and begged for admission. The mother of the Sun opened the door, and was astonished at beholding a mortal from the distant earthly shores, and wept with pity when she heard of all she had suffered. Then, having promised to ask her son about the Princess's husband, she hid her in the cellar, so that the Sun might notice nothing on his return home, for he was always in a bad temper when he came in at night.

The next day the Princess feared that things would not go well with her, for the Sun had noticed that someone from the other world had been in the palace. But his mother had soothed him with soft words, assuring him that this was not so. So the Princess took heart when she saw how kindly she was treated, and asked, "But how in the world is it possible for the Sun to be angry? He is so beautiful and so good to mortals."

"This is how it happens," replied the Sun's mother. "In the morning when he stands at the gates of paradise he is happy, and smiles on the whole world, but during the day he gets cross, because he sees all the evil deeds of men, and that is why his heat becomes so scorching, but in the evening he is both sad and angry, for he stands at the gates of death. That is his usual course. From there he comes back here."

She then told the Princess that she had asked about her husband, but that her son had replied that he knew nothing about him, and that her only hope was to go and inquire of the Wind.

Before the Princess left the mother of the Sun gave her a roast chicken to eat, and advised her to take great care of the bones, which she did, wrapping them up in a bundle. She then threw away her second pair of shoes, which were quite worn out, and with her child on her arm and her staff in her hand, she set forth on her way to the Wind.

In these wanderings she met with even greater difficulties than before, for she came upon one mountain of flints after another, out of which tongues of fire would flame up. She passed through woods which had never been trodden by human foot, and had to cross fields of ice and avalanches of snow. The poor woman nearly died of these hardships, but she kept a brave heart, and at length she reached an enormous cave in the side of a mountain. This was where the Wind lived. There was a little door in the railing in front of the cave, and here the Princess knocked and begged for admission. The mother of the Wind had pity on her and took her in, that she might rest a little. Here too she was hidden away, so that the Wind might not notice her.

The next morning the mother of the Wind told her that her husband was living in a thick wood, so thick that no axe had been able to cut a way through it. He had built himself a sort of house by placing trunks of trees together and fastening them with withes and here he lived alone, shunning humankind.

After the mother of the Wind had given the Princess a chicken to eat, and had warned her to take care of the bones, she advised her to go by the Milky Way, which at night lies across the sky, and to wander on till she reached her goal.

Having thanked the old woman with tears in her eyes for her hospitality, and for the good news she had given her, the Princess set out on her journey and rested neither night nor day, so great was her longing to see her husband again. On and on she walked until her last pair of shoes fell in pieces. So she threw them away and went on with bare feet, not heeding the bogs nor the thorns that wounded her, nor the stones that bruised her.

At last she reached a beautiful green meadow on the edge of a wood. Her heart was cheered by the sight of the flowers and the soft cool grass, and she sat down and rested for a little. But hearing the birds chirping to their mates among the trees made her think with longing of her husband, and she wept bitterly, and taking her child in her arms, and her bundle of chicken bones on her shoulder, she entered the wood.

For three days and three nights she struggled through it, but could find nothing. She was quite worn out with weariness and hunger, and even her staff was no further help to her, for in her many wanderings it had become quite blunted. She almost gave up in despair, but made one last great effort, and suddenly in a thicket she came upon the sort of house that the mother of the Wind had described. It had no windows, and the door was up in the roof. Round the house she went, in search of steps, but could find none. What was she to do? How was she to get in? She thought and thought, and tried in vain to climb up to the door. Then suddenly she thought of the chicken bones that she had dragged all that weary way, and she said to herself, "They would not all have told me to take such good care of these bones if they had not had some good reason for doing so. Perhaps now, in my hour of need, they may be of use to me."

So she took the bones out of her bundle, and having thought for a moment, she placed the two ends together. To her surprise they stuck tight; then she added the other bones, till she had two long poles the height of the house; these she placed against the wall, at a distance of a yard from one another. Across them she placed the other bones, piece by piece, like the steps of a ladder. As soon as one step was finished she stood upon it and made the next one, and then the next, till she was close to the door.

But just as she got near the top she noticed that there were no bones left for the last rung of the ladder. What was she to do? Without that last step the whole ladder was useless. She must have lost one of the bones. Then suddenly an idea came to her. Taking a knife she chopped off her little finger, and placing it on the last step, it stuck as the bones had done. The ladder was complete, and with her child on her arm she entered the door of the house. Here she found everything in perfect order. Having taken some food, she laid the child down to sleep in a trough that was on the floor, and sat down herself to rest.

When her husband, the Pig, came back to his house, he was startled by what he saw. At first he could not believe his eyes, and stared at the ladder of bones, and at the little finger on the top of it. He felt that some fresh magic must be at work, and in his terror he almost turned away from the house, but then a better idea came to him, and he changed himself into a dove, so that no witchcraft could have power over him, and flew into the room without touching the ladder. Here he found a woman rocking a child. At the sight of her, looking so changed by all that she had suffered for his sake, his heart was moved by such love and longing and by so great a pity that he suddenly became a man.

The Princess stood up when she saw him, and her heart beat with fear, for she did not know him. But when he had told her who he was, in her great joy she forgot all her sufferings, and they seemed like nothing to her. He was a very handsome man, as straight as a fir tree. They sat down together and she told him all her adventures, and he wept with pity at the tale. And then he told her his own history.

"I am a King's son. Once when my father was fighting against some dragons, who were the scourge of our country, I slew the youngest dragon. His mother, who was a witch, cast a spell over me and changed me into a Pig. It was she who in the disguise of an old woman gave you the thread to bind round my foot. So that instead of the three days that had to run before the spell was broken, I was forced to remain a Pig for three more years. Now that we have suffered for each other, and have found each other again, let us forget the past."

And in their joy they kissed one another.

Next morning they set out early to return to his father's kingdom. Great was the rejoicing of all the people when they saw him and his wife, and his father and his mother embraced them both, and there was feasting in the palace for three days and three nights.

Then they set out to see her father. The old King nearly went out of his mind with joy at beholding his daughter again. When she had told him all her adventures, he said to her, "Did I not tell you that I was quite sure that the creature who wooed and won you as his wife had not been born a Pig? You see, my child, how wise you were in doing what I told you."

And as the King was old and had no heirs, he put them on the throne in his place. And they ruled as only kings rule who have suffered many things. And if they are not dead they are still living and ruling happily.

Gullinbursti, the Golden-Bristled Boar

A Norse Tale

This tale is my own versions of a traditional Norse legend taken from various sources in my own collection of folk and fairy tales. Gullinbursti, the Golden-Bristled Boar, originates specifically in the Prose Edda (13th century) written by Snorri Sturluson, though it almost certainly draws on older oral traditions from the Viking Age.

In the days when gods still walked freely across the Nine Realms, there came a time when Loki, the trickster, found himself in trouble, as often he did. He had angered the Lady Sif by cutting off her golden hair while she slept. Thor, her husband, swore he would break every bone in Loki's body unless he restored it.

Loki, sly as ever, promised to set things right. He hurried down into the deep halls of Svartalfheim, where the dwarfs lived, the greatest smiths of all the worlds. There he went to the sons of Ivaldi, a master craftsmen, and begged them to fashion for Sif new hair of gold that would grow upon her head as if it were her own.

The dwarfs agreed, but they were proud of their skill, and Loki, ever eager for mischief, boasted to other smiths, the brothers Brokkr and Sindri, that no one could rival the sons of Ivaldi. Brokkr laughed in his face.

"Our work is finer than theirs. We will make treasures greater than anything they can shape. If we fail, I will give you my head."

Loki grinned at that wager, for he thought he had already won.

So Brokkr and Sindri set to their forge. Sindri placed gold upon the fire and told Brokkr to keep the bellows blowing, never stopping, or the work would be spoiled. Loki, fearing their success, turned himself into a biting fly and stung Brokkr on the hand. Still, Brokkr held firm, and out from the forge came Sif's new golden hair, shining like sunlight.

Next, Sindri placed a piece of pigskin upon the fire. Again he warned Brokkr: "Keep the bellows strong." Loki, frantic now, stung Brokkr's neck until the blood ran into his eyes, but Brokkr did not falter. From the fire came a living boar, bristling with golden hairs that gleamed like firebrands. This was Gullinbursti.

Lastly, Sindri placed iron in the forge, and again Loki stung Brokkr, this time on the eyelid, so that blood nearly blinded him. For an instant he faltered, and the work was marred. Yet from the flames they drew forth a mighty hammer, short in handle but heavy beyond measure. This was Mjölnir, the weapon that would one day defend Asgard against giants and doom itself.

When the gifts were laid before the gods, it was Freyr, lord of the sun, harvest, and peace, who received Gullinbursti. The boar stamped the ground, and golden sparks flew from his bristles, lighting the dark like torches. No beast was swifter, for he could run across earth, sea, and even through the air, never tiring, as swift as the wind itself.

Freyr laughed with joy. "With this boar, I need fear no night, no shadow, no enemy who thinks to outrun me. His light shall be as the sun upon the fields, and his strength shall be mine in war."

And so it was. Freyr rode Gullinbursti into battle, the boar's golden mane blazing across the horizon. Wherever he passed, crops ripened, and foes trembled at the sight. Some say that even in death, when Baldr's funeral ship was launched, it was Gullinbursti who drew Freyr's chariot to the pyre, his bristles shining bright enough to honour the fallen god.

Thus was Gullinbursti born of fire and cunning, a boar of unearthly beauty and terror, forged by dwarfs, saved from Loki's mischief, and made the pride of Freyr. His golden light cut through every darkness, and his name is still spoken as one of the great wonders of the old Norse world.

The Bear, The Boar, And The Fox

A Russian Tale

This tale is adapted from a story told by Louise Seymour Houghton in her book The Russian Grandmother's Wonder Tales, published by Charles Scribner's Sons, London & New York, in 1906.

Louise Seymour Houghton (1838–1920) was an American writer, translator, and folklorist who helped introduce Old World fairy tales and folk traditions to English-speaking audiences. She is best known for presenting Russian folktales, such as stories of Baba Yaga, firebirds, and enchanted princes, adapted in a style accessible to children while preserving their distinctly Slavic flavour.

A Bear, a Boar, and a Fox once went into partnership to till a field and raise some wheat, so that they might earn their bread honestly.

The Boar said, "I will break into a granary and steal the seed, and with my snout I will plough up the field."

"I will be the sower," said the Bear.

The Fox added, "I will spread the earth over the seed with my tail."

195

So the field was ploughed and the seed sown. By and by harvest-time arrived, and the friends took counsel together as to the reaping.

The Boar said, "I will cut the grain."

The Bear replied, "I will bind the sheaves."

And the Fox said, "I will glean the scattered ears."

The grain was cut and the sheaves set up. The next thing was the threshing.

The Boar said, "I will provide the threshing-floor."

"I will carry the sheaves," said the Bear. "And will do the threshing into the bargain."

"I'll shake out the sheaves," said the Boar, "and break off the ears from the stalks."

"I will clear away the chaff with my tail," said the Fox.

"I will winnow the grain," said the Boar, "and separate the straw from the wheat."

The Bear added, "And I will attend to the dividing."

And so the grain was threshed.

Then the Bear started to do the dividing, but he was neither fair nor honest, for he gave the Boar all the straw and kept all the grain for himself, not leaving the least thing for the Fox. At this the Fox flew into a rage and threatened them both with the law, saying he would bring the emperor's officer to divide it all fairly and squarely.

Away he went for the officer, leaving the Boar and the Bear greatly terrified. Said the Bear to the Boar, "Just bury yourself in the straw, my child, while I clamber up into that pear-tree over there." The Boar at once vanished under the straw, while the Bear scrambled up into the pear-tree.

Meanwhile the Fox set out, and on the way he met a Cat, whom he invited to come and hunt mice with him upon a certain threshing-floor.

The Cat gladly accepted the invitation, for she full well knew that there are plenty of mice in a threshing-floor, but on the way she kept hunting birds in the bushes along the roadside. The Bear, who was watching from the pear-tree, spied her from afar, and called down to the Boar, "We are in a pretty scrape, dear Boar, for here comes Master Fox and a fearful monster with him. He wears the fur coat of a Marten and is killing birds upon the wing all along the way."

By this time the Bear lost sight of the Cat, which had reached the threshing-floor under cover of the grass, and was creeping about in the straw in search of mice. Full of curiosity, the Boar stuck his head out a little way to see what was going on, when the Cat, mistaking his snout for a mouse, sprang forward and buried her claws in it. At this the Boar gave a fearful grunt, and rushed frantically into a neighbouring stream, while the Bear, who, from the uproar, concluded that the Cat had killed the Boar and would seize him next, tumbled headlong from the pear-tree in terror, and breaking his neck by the fall, perished miserably.

So Master Fox got all the grain and the straw into the bargain.

The Hare And The Pig

An Indian Tale

This is my version of a tale told by Kate Douglas Wiggin and Nora Archibald Smith in their book, The Talking Beasts, published by Houghton Mifflin Company, New York & Boston, in 1911. This tale is based on an anecdote by a man named Raju.

Kate Douglas Wiggin (1856–1923) and her sister Nora Archibald Smith (1859–1934) were American authors and educators known for their influential work in children's literature and early childhood education.

In the old days, when the animals of the forest still quarrelled like children and asked the trickster-fox to settle their disputes, there lived a boastful Hare and a stubborn Pig.

The Hare was quick and restless, always leaping and darting about, forever speaking of his speed. "No one can out-jump me!" he would boast. "Why, I could leap over rivers and streams with hardly a splash!"

The Pig, who was slow but thick-skinned, snorted at this. "Speed is nothing. Strength is everything! I may not be quick on my feet, but when I leap, I leap with all my weight. Let us see who is the greater!"

So one morning they came upon a wide ditch at the edge of the paddy fields. It was dry and deep, and the Hare's whiskers quivered with excitement.

"Here is the place to prove ourselves," said the Hare.

"Agreed!" said the Pig.

The Hare crouched low, kicked his hind legs, and sprang with all his might. He sailed across the air, so near to victory, but alas, he landed just one inch short. Down he tumbled into the ditch, sprawling in the dust.

The Pig grunted and took his turn. He lumbered back a few steps, charged forward, and gave a mighty jump. But his leap was heavy and clumsy, and he crashed far short of the Hare, and into the ditch he went as well.

Now both sat there, Hare nursing his pride, Pig rubbing his snout, and still they argued.

"I leapt farther than you!" cried the Hare.

"But I leapt with more force!" grunted the Pig.

"And so I am the better animal!"

"No, I am the better animal!"

A sly Fox had been watching all along from the bank above. They turned to him, their quarrel still hot.

"Brother Fox," they said together, "you have seen our leaps with your own eyes. Tell us truly, which of us is superior, and which inferior?"

The Fox licked his lips, twitched his tail, and grinned down at them.

"Superior? Inferior? Bah! You are both in the ditch. What more can I say?"

And with that, he trotted off, leaving the Hare and the Pig to their squabble, both stuck in the same dust-hole.

So the village folk say, "In trying to prove who is greater, many end up in the same ditch."

The Swineherd

A Danish Tale

This tale is adapted from a story told by Hans Christian Andersen in the book Fairy Tales of Hans Christian Andersen, published by George H. Doran Co., New York, in 1914.

While Andersen is often grouped with collectors like the Brothers Grimm, who recorded existing folk tales, Andersen crafted new stories inspired by folk motifs but deeply personal in tone and theme. Tales like The Little Mermaid, The Ugly Duckling, The Snow Queen, and The Emperor's New Clothes were his own inventions, blending childlike wonder with subtle social criticism and emotional depth.

There was once a poor Prince, who had a kingdom. His kingdom was very small, but still quite large enough to marry upon, and he wished to marry.

It was certainly rather cool of him to say to the Emperor's daughter, "Will you have me?" But so he did, for his name was renowned far and wide, and there were a hundred princesses who would have answered, "Yes!" and "Thank you kindly." We shall see what this princess said.

Listen!

It happened that where the Prince's father lay buried, there grew a rose tree, a most beautiful rose tree, which blossomed only once in every five years, and even then bore only one flower, but that was a rose! It smelt so sweet that all cares and sorrows were forgotten by anyone who inhaled its fragrance.

And furthermore, the Prince had a nightingale, who could sing in such a manner that it seemed as though all sweet melodies dwelt in her little throat. So the Princess was to have the rose, and the nightingale, and they were accordingly put into large silver caskets, and sent to her.

The Emperor had them brought into a large hall, where the Princess was playing at "Visiting," with the ladies of the court, and when she saw the caskets with the presents, she clapped her hands for joy.

"Ah, if it were but a little pussy-cat!" said she, but the rose tree, with its beautiful rose came to view.

"Oh, how prettily it is made!" said all the court ladies.

"It is more than pretty," said the Emperor, "it is charming!"

But the Princess touched it, and was almost ready to cry.

"Fie, papa!" said she. "It is not made at all, it is natural!"

"Let us see what is in the other casket, before we get into a bad humour," said the Emperor. So the nightingale came forth and sang so delightfully that at first no one could say anything ill of her.

"Superbe! Charmant!" exclaimed the ladies, for they all used to chatter French, each one worse than her neighbour.

"How much the bird reminds me of the musical box that belonged to our blessed Empress," said an old knight. "Oh yes! These are the same tones, the same execution."

"Yes! Yes!" said the Emperor, and he wept like a child at the remembrance.

"I will still hope that it is not a real bird," said the Princess.

"Yes, it is a real bird," said those who had brought it. "Well then let the bird fly," said the Princess; and she positively refused to see the Prince.

However, he was not to be discouraged, he daubed his face over brown and black, pulled his cap over his ears, and knocked at the door.

"Good day to my lord, the Emperor!" said he. "Can I have employment at the palace?"

"Why, yes," said the Emperor. "I want someone to take care of the pigs, for we have a great many of them."

So the Prince was appointed "Imperial Swineherd." He had a dirty little room close by the pigsty, and there he sat the whole day, and worked. By the evening he had made a pretty little kitchen-pot. Little bells were hung all round it; and when the pot was boiling, these bells tinkled in the most charming manner, and played the old melody,

"Ach! Du lieber Augustin, Alles ist weg, weg, weg!"

But what was still more curious, was the fact that whoever held his finger in the steam of the kitchen-pot, immediately smelt all the dishes that were cooking on every hearth in the city, and this, you see, was something quite different from the rose.

Now the Princess happened to walk that way, and when she heard the tune, she stood quite still, and seemed pleased, for she could play "Lieber Augustine". It was the only piece she knew, and she played it with one finger.

"Why there is my piece," said the Princess. "That swineherd must certainly have been well educated! Go in and ask him the price of the instrument."

So one of the court-ladies ran in, however, she drew on wooden slippers first.

"What will you take for the kitchen-pot?" said the lady.

"I will have ten kisses from the Princess," said the swineherd.

"Yes, indeed!" said the lady.

"I cannot sell it for less," rejoined the swineherd.

"He is an impudent fellow!" said the Princess, and she walked on, but when she had gone a little way, the bells tinkled so prettily again.

"Ach! Du lieber Augustin, Alles ist weg, weg, weg!"

"Stay," said the Princess. "Ask him if he will have ten kisses from the ladies of my court."

"No, thank you!" said the swineherd. "Ten kisses from the Princess, or I keep the kitchen-pot myself."

"That must not be, either!" said the Princess. "But all of you, my ladies, stand before me that no one may see us."

And the court-ladies placed themselves in front of her, and spread out their dresses. The swineherd got ten kisses, and the Princess got the kitchen-pot.

That was delightful! The pot was boiling the whole evening, and the whole of the following day. They knew perfectly well what was cooking at every fire throughout the city, from the chamberlain's to the cobbler's, and the court-ladies danced and clapped their hands.

"We know who has soup, and who has pancakes for dinner today, who has cutlets, and who has eggs. How interesting!"

"Yes, but keep my secret, for I am an Emperor's daughter."

The swineherd, that is to say, the Prince, for no one knew that he was anything other than an ill-favoured swineherd, let not a day pass without working at something. He at last constructed a rattle, which, when it was swung round, played all the waltzes and jig tunes, which have ever been heard since the creation of the world.

"Ah, that is superbe!" said the Princess when she passed by. "I have never heard prettier compositions! Go in and ask him the price of the instrument, but mind, he shall have no more kisses!"

"He will have a hundred kisses from the Princess!" said the lady who had been to ask.

"I think he is not in his right senses!" said the Princess, and walked on, but when she had gone a little way, she stopped again. "One must encourage art," she said, "I am the Emperor's daughter. Tell him he shall, as on yesterday, have ten kisses from me, and may take the rest from the ladies of the court."

"Oh, but we should not like that at all!" they said.

"What are you muttering?" asked the Princess. "If I can kiss him, surely you can. Remember that you owe everything to me." So the ladies were obliged to go to him again.

"A hundred kisses from the Princess," said he, "or else let everyone keep his own!"

"Oh, stand round!" she said, and all the ladies stood round her whilst the kissing was going on.

"Why is there such a crowd close by the pigsty?" said the Emperor, who happened just then to step out on the balcony. He rubbed his eyes, and put on his spectacles. "They are the ladies of the court. I must go down and see what they are about!" So he pulled up his slippers at the heel, for he had trodden them down.

As soon as he had got into the court-yard, he moved very softly, and the ladies were so much engrossed with counting the kisses, that all might go on fairly, that they did not perceive the Emperor. He rose on his tiptoes.

"What is all this?" he said, when he saw what was going on, and he boxed the Princess's ears with his slipper, just as the swineherd was taking the eighty-sixth kiss.

"March out!" said the Emperor, for he was very angry, and both Princess and swineherd were thrust out of the city.

The Princess now stood and wept, the swineherd scolded, and the rain poured down.

"Alas! Unhappy creature that I am!" said the Princess. "If I had but married the handsome young Prince! Ah! how unfortunate I am!"

And the swineherd went behind a tree, washed the black and brown colour from his face, threw off his dirty clothes, and stepped forth in his princely robes. He looked so noble that the Princess could not help bowing before him.

"I have come to despise you," he said. "You would not accept an honourable prince. You could not value the rose or the nightingale, yet you were eager to kiss a swineherd for the sake of a worthless trinket. You are getting exactly what you deserve."

With that, he returned to his own small kingdom and slammed the palace door in her face. Now she, at last, had reason to sing "Ach! du lieber Augustin, Alles ist weg, weg, weg!"

How The Boars Killed The Rakshasa

A Sri Lankan Tale

This tale is my version of an original tale by Henry Parker in his book, Village Folk-Tales of Ceylon, Volume 1, published by Luzac And Co., London, in 1910. This tale was related to Henry Parker by Rodiya, of the North-western Province.

Henry Parker was a British civil servant and folklorist who worked in colonial Sri Lanka (then Ceylon) during the late 19th and early 20th centuries. Deeply interested in the island's culture, Parker collected and translated a wealth of Sinhalese folklore, legends, and village beliefs, preserving them in English for a wider audience. His most notable work, Village Folk-Tales of Ceylon (1890–1910), is a three-volume collection that remains a significant resource on South Asian oral traditions.

Long ago, beside a great city there stretched a deep, wild jungle. In that jungle lived a sow, heavy with young. One day, as her time came, she wandered to the high ground near a village and gave birth to a single boar.

The people of the house who found him pitied the creature. They fed him scraps, gave him water, and raised him as their own. The boar grew strong, bigger than any in the village, and yet, as he grew older, a restless spirit filled him.

"I am no tame animal to eat men's leftovers," he thought. "I must return to the wild."

So he left the village and entered the jungle. There, he found other wild boars living in fear. A Rakshasa, one of the man-eating demons, had made the jungle his hunting ground, devouring the strongest among them.

The village boar listened and then said, "Friends, I have a plan. If you do as I say, we may outwit the Rakshasa."

The others gathered close. "Tell us your trick," they begged.

He told them this, "Dig two great pits, as deep as wells. At the bottom, join them with a tunnel. I will stand above the middle of the wells, and the rest of you must gather around me. When the Rakshasa comes, copy everything he does."

So the boars dug as he commanded, and when they were ready, they waited.

The Rakshasa came at his usual time, climbing upon a rock to glare down at the herd. He bared his teeth and made terrible faces at them. But this time, all the boars made the same faces back. He swelled his chest to frighten them, and they puffed out theirs. He roared so loud the forest shook, and the boars roared back, all together, as if they were an army.

The Rakshasa was shaken. "These creatures are turning into demons themselves," he thought, and in his fear he fled to the Lion King of the jungle.

But the Lion scolded him. "Shame on you! You, a Rakshasa, fleeing from pigs? Go back and finish what you began!"

Ashamed, the Rakshasa returned the next day. The boars bristled and stamped, ready for the plan.

The village boar said, "When the Rakshasa leaps at me, I will dive into the well. He will follow, but I will escape through the tunnel to the other side. Then you must fall upon him together."

And so it happened. The Rakshasa sprang, the boar slipped into the well, and the demon tumbled in after him, but the village boar was already gone through the tunnel. The Rakshasa found himself surrounded by the wild boars, who tore him apart and left nothing but bones.

When it was done, the boars asked, "Who else rules over us now?"

The great boar replied, "There is still the Lion King."

So together they marched to his den. But the Lion, seeing them coming in a fierce herd, scrambled up a tree to escape. The boars set to work with their tusks, gnawing and breaking the roots until the tree crashed to the ground. The Lion leapt away, but they chased him through the forest, caught him, and slew him too.

And from that day, the boars of that jungle feared neither Rakshasa nor Lion, for with wit and unity they had overthrown them both.

The Story Of The Pig-Trough

A Welsh Tale

This tale is adapted from a story told by Peter Henry Emerson in his book Fairy-Tales & Other Stories, published by D. Nutt, London in 1894Some stuff about the people

Peter Henry Emerson (1856–1936) was a British photographer and writer, best known for pioneering naturalistic photography in the late 19th century. Rejecting the stiff, staged style of Victorian studio portraits, he championed photography as a fine art that should capture life as it truly appeared, especially rural landscapes and the everyday work of peasants in East Anglia. His influential books, such as Life and Landscape on the Norfolk Broads (1886), combined evocative images with prose to celebrate simple country life.

At the beginning of the nineteenth century, Dafydd Hughes went as a military substitute in place of a rich farmer's son. He got £80, a watch, and a suit of clothes.

His mother was loath to let him go, and when he joined his regiment, she followed him from Amlwch to Pwllheli to try and buy him off. He would not hear of it.

"Mother," he said, "the whole of Anglesey would not keep me, I want to be off, and see the world."

The regiment was quartered in Edinboro', and Hughes married the daughter of the burgess with whom he was billeted.

Then, leaving a small son, as hostage to the grandparents, they went to Ireland, and Hughes and his wife were billeted on a pork-butcher's family in Dublin.

One day, the mother of the pork-butcher, an old granny, told them she had seen the fairies.

"Last night, as I was in bed, I saw a bright light come in, and afterwards a troop of little angels. They danced all over my bed, and they played and sang music, oh, the sweetest music ever I heard. I lay and watched them and listened. Bye-and-bye the light went out and the music stopped, and I saw them no more. I regretted losing the music very much.

"But directly after another smaller light appeared, and a tall dark man came up to my bed, and with something in his hand he tapped me on the temple. It felt like someone drawing a sharp pin across my temple then he went too. In the morning my pillow was covered with blood.

"I thought, and then I knew I had moved the pig's trough and put it in the fairies' path and the fairies were angered, and the king of the fairies punished me for it."

She moved the trough back to its old place the next day and received no more visits from the wee folk.

A Pig Witched

A Welsh Tale

This tale is adapted from a story told by Elias Owen in his book Welsh Folk-Lore, published by Elliot Stock, London, in 1896.

Elias Owen (1833–1899), a Welsh clergyman and folklorist, is best remembered for his book Welsh Folk-Lore (1896), which gathered together tales of fairies, charms, superstitions, and ghost stories from across Wales. While serving as an Anglican curate, he openly collected and preserved beliefs that many of his fellow clergy dismissed as "heathen" or dangerous remnants of paganism. Even more curiously, his own life ended tragically and mysteriously. He died by suicide in a well at his rectory, a fate that later cast a haunting shadow over his reputation as a collector of eerie tales and gave his folklore work an uncanny aura of belonging to the very ghostly world he wrote about.

In the old market town of Beaumaris, where farmers and traders came in from every valley and hillside of Anglesey, there lived a woman who kept pigs. She was known for being sharp in her bargains, and her beasts were always plump and well-fed.

One market day she sold a fine young pig to a man called Dick y Green. Dick was a familiar figure in Beaumaris, broad-shouldered, rough in speech, and known to be quick to complain if ever he thought he had been cheated. The woman sold him the pig fair and square and went home well pleased, though she sold no other animals that day.

The following market day she returned to Beaumaris. As soon as she stepped into the square, there was Dick waiting for her, his face dark as thunder.

"Woman," he said, "the pig you sold me is bewitched. It eats nothing, stirs little, and groans like a dying man. You must come with me and undo the curse."

Now the woman was startled, for in those days folk in Anglesey feared curses and charms as much as steel or fire. She followed Dick back to his farm without protest. When they came to the sty, there lay the pig, restless and low, its eyes dull as stones.

"What am I to do now, Dick?" asked the woman.

"Lay your hand upon his back," Dick told her, "and draw it down seven times. Each time you pass your hand, say these words: Rhad Duw arnat ti, 'The blessing of God be upon thee.'"

So she did as he said. Once, twice, three times, until seven times she had stroked the pig's bristly back, speaking the blessing with every stroke. The pig gave a great snort, as if some weight had been lifted, and shuffled to its feet.

"There now," said Dick, his face brightening. "The curse is broken. I'll fetch physic for him, and he'll soon be sound again."

And indeed, within days the pig was feeding well and growing strong, and Dick had no more complaints.

Folk in Beaumaris say the woman went on selling pigs for many years after, but she always remembered the day she was called upon to speak a blessing over a bewitched beast. Some say still that it was not witchcraft at all but Dick y Green's cunning way of getting free help from a sharp-tongued pig-seller. Yet others insist there are stranger things in the hills of Wales than pigs that sicken without cause.

The Sow and the Crow

An English Tale

This tale is my own versions of a traditional Norse legend taken from various sources in my own collection of folk and fairy tales.

The tale of The Sow and the Crow has its roots in the ancient Greek fable tradition, attributed to Babrius, a 2nd-century Greek fabulist who versified many Aesopic tales. Babrius's versions often expanded simple fables into short poetic narratives. Later, in the medieval period, his fables (and those of related collections like Phaedrus) circulated widely across Europe in Latin and vernacular retellings, often picked up by monks and moralists as teaching stories.

In a village on the edge of a forest, there lived a sow who was forever busy with her little ones. She was a mother many times over, and every spring her pen filled with squealing piglets. They tumbled in the mud, rooted about for scraps, and nuzzled close to their mother's side. The sow took pride in her brood, though she was always weary, for keeping so many children fed was no small task.

One day, as the sow lay resting in the shade after a long morning of rooting, a crow perched on the fence post above her. The crow tilted its head, black eyes gleaming with mischief, and croaked out a laugh.

"Well, well, what a sight! Every year you fill the yard with children, and yet not one of them is remarkable. Look at them, muddy little creatures, noisy and common. Wouldn't it be better to have one fine chick than a dozen dirty piglets?"

The piglets squeaked in alarm, but the sow only raised her head slowly and looked at the crow. Her eyes were tired, but they burned with quiet strength.

"You mock me, black-feather," she said, "but tell me this, what becomes of your chicks, hatched high in your nest? They learn to snatch, to steal, to pick at the dead. They live on scraps and theft, flying from one place to the next. Is that a noble life?"

The crow ruffled its feathers and let out another harsh caw.

"My children may not be many," the sow continued, "but they live honestly. They grow strong on the food I find, and they harm no one. They do not take what is not theirs. They do not live by cunning or carrion. My piglets may be plain, but they are honest, and there is honour in that."

The crow fell silent at her words. For though he would never admit it, he knew her truth cut deeper than any insult. He flapped his wings and flew off across the fields, leaving the sow and her brood in peace.

The little pigs, crowding close to their mother, asked, "Why did the crow laugh at us, Mama?"

The sow nuzzled them and said, "Because some creatures think that having fewer children, or children who look fine, makes them better. But what matters is not how they look or how many there are. What matters is how they live."

And from that day on, the piglets squealed with a bit more pride, and the crow did not come to taunt them again, for boasting about beauty or number means little, what matters is living with honesty.

The Pigs

A Danish Tale

This tale is adapted from a story told by Hans Christian Andersen in his book What the Moon Saw: and Other Tales, published by George Routledge & Sons, Ltd., London, in 1866.

One unusual thing about Hans Christian Andersen is that, despite being adored worldwide for his fairy tales, he was notoriously anxious and eccentric in his personal life. He travelled with a rope in his luggage wherever he went, in case he needed to escape from a burning hotel room, and he was terrified of being buried alive, so much so that he left written instructions that his pulse must be thoroughly checked before his burial. Even in his friendships, he could be awkward: during his infamous visit to Charles Dickens's home, he overstayed his welcome by weeks, leaving Dickens so exasperated that he scrawled on the guest-room mirror, "Hans Andersen slept in this room for five weeks, which seemed to the family AGES!"

Charles Dickens once told us about a pig, and since that time we are in a good humour if we only hear one grunt. St. Antony took the pig under his protection, and when we think of the prodigal son we always associate with him the idea of feeding swine, and it was in front of a pig-sty that a certain carriage stopped in Sweden, about which I am going to talk. The farmer had his pig-sty built out towards the high road, close by his house, and it was a wonderful pig-sty. It was an old state carriage. The seats had been taken out and the wheels taken off, and so the body of the old coach lay on the ground, and four pigs were shut up inside it. I wonder if these were the first that had ever been there? That point could not certainly be determined, but that it had been a real state coach everything bore witness, even to the damask rag that hung down from the roof. Everything spoke of better days.

We came back in autumn. The coach was there still, but the pigs were gone. They were playing the grand lords out in the woods. Blossoms and leaves were gone from all the trees, and storm and rain ruled, and gave them neither peace nor rest, and the birds of passage had flown.

"The beautiful has departed! This was the glorious green wood, but the song of the birds and the warm sunshine are gone! gone!" Thus said the mournful voice that creaked in the lofty branches of the trees, and it sounded like a deep-drawn sigh, a sigh from the bosom of the wild rose tree, and of him who sat there. It was the rose king. Do you know him? He is all beard, the finest reddish-green beard, and he is easily recognised. Go up to the wild rose bushes, and when in autumn all the flowers have faded from them, and only the wild hips remain, you will often find under them a great red-green moss flower, and that is the rose king. A little green leaf grows up out of his head, and that's his feather. He is the only man of his kind on the rose bush; and he it was who sighed.

"Gone! gone! The beautiful is gone! The roses have faded, and the leaves fall down! It's wet here! it's boisterous here! The birds who used to sing are dumb, and the pigs go out hunting for acorns, and the pigs are the lords of the forest!"

The nights were cold and the days were misty, but, for all that, the raven sat on the branch and sang, "Good! good!" Raven and crow sat on the high bough, and they had a large family, who all said, "Good! good!" and the majority is always right.

Under the high trees, in the hollow, was a great puddle, and here the pigs reclined, great and small. They found the place so inexpressibly lovely! "Oui! Oui!" they all exclaimed. That was all the French they knew, but even that was something; and they were so clever and so fat!

The old ones lay quite still, and reflected, while the young ones were very busy, and were not quiet a moment. One little porker had a twist in his tail like a ring, and this ring was his mother's pride. She thought all the rest were looking at the ring, and thinking only of the ring, but that they were not doing. They were thinking of themselves and of what was useful, and what was the use of the wood. They had always heard that the acorns they ate grew at the roots of the trees, and accordingly they had grubbed up the ground, but there came quite a little pig - it's always the young ones who come out with their new-fangled notions - who declared that the acorns fell down from the branches, for one had just fallen down on his head, and the idea had struck him at once, and afterwards he had made observations, and now was quite certain on the point.

The old ones put their heads together. "Umph!" they said, "umph! The glory has departed. The twittering of the birds is all over. We want fruit. Whatever's good to eat is good, and we eat everything."

"Oui! Oui!" chimed in all the rest.

But the mother now looked at her little porker, the one with the ring in his tail, "One must not overlook the beautiful," she said.

"Good! good!" cried the crow, and flew down from the tree to try and get an appointment as nightingale, for someone must be appointed, and the crow obtained the office directly.

"Gone! gone!" sighed the rose king. "All the beautiful is gone!"

It was boisterous, it was grey, cold, and windy, and through the forest and over the field swept the rain in long dark streaks. Where is the bird who sang, where are the flowers upon the meadow, and the sweet berries of the wood? Gone! gone!

Then a light gleamed from the forester's house. It was lit up like a star, and threw its long ray among the trees. A song sounded forth out of the house! Beautiful children played there round the old grandfather. He sat with the Bible on his knee, and read of the Creator and of a better world, and spoke of spring that would return, of the forest that would array itself in fresh green, of the roses that would bloom, the nightingale that would sing, and of the beautiful that would reign in its glory again.

But the rose king heard it not, for he sat in the cold, damp weather, and sighed, "Gone! gone!" And the pigs were the lords of the forest, and the old mother sow looked proudly at her little porker with the twist in his tail.

"There is always somebody who has a soul for the beautiful!" she said.

The Pig in the Meadow

A Classic Fable

This tale is my own version of a traditional medieval tale taken from various sources in my own collection of traditional folk and fairy tales. It is a variant of the tale, The Swine And The Sheep, told earlier in this book.

The Pig in the Meadow is a medieval European fable, with its roots in the same tradition as Aesop's fables and later Latin and medieval sermon collections. It shows up in different guises, usually contrasting the noisy squeals of a pig with the quieter behaviour of other farm animals like sheep or cows.

The earliest forms appear in Aesop's corpus (6th century BCE Greece) under fables such as The Pig and the Sheep or The Swine and the Sheep, where the pig squeals when seized, while the sheep do not, and the pig explains that he is being taken for his life, not just his wool.

In the Middle Ages, this fable was retold in Latin bestiaries, sermon-stories, and medieval household collections.

Once, in the green meadows beyond a small village, the beasts of the farm lived together in uneasy company. The cows grazed quietly, the sheep nibbled close to the ground, and the horses, proud and strong, flicked their tails as they stood in the sun.

But the pigs, ah, the pigs were different. They rooted noisily in the earth, squealing and grunting at every turn, as though the whole meadow belonged to them alone.

One bright morning, the farmer's wife came with her basket to lead away a fattened pig for the market. At once the chosen pig began to shriek and squeal so loudly that the birds fled from the hedges and the other animals lifted their heads in alarm.

"Help! Murder! I am undone!" cried the pig, twisting and struggling. His cries rang out across the meadow as though he were being dragged to some terrible doom.

The sheep, chewing calmly, spoke at last. "Why must you make such a fuss? When the farmer takes us, we go quietly enough. A little wool is shorn, and we are returned to the meadow. Do you hear us bleating and bellowing as you do?"

The cows agreed. "We too are handled often, our milk taken, our yokes fitted, our hides brushed. We go patiently. Why must you shriek so, brother pig?"

The pig writhed in the farmer's grasp, his eyes wild, and answered through his squeals:

"You fools! When he takes you, he does not take your lives. He only shears your wool or drains your milk, and back you go to graze another day. But when he takes me, it is for the knife. It is for my flesh and my blood. Do you wonder, then, that I scream?"

At this the meadow grew silent. The cows lowered their heads, the horses stamped uneasily, and the sheep no longer dared to laugh at their noisy neighbour. For in his cries, they heard the sound of a creature who knew the weight of his fate.

And the pig's squeals carried on, long after he was led away, echoing as a lesson in the hearts of the beasts who had once thought him foolish. It is easy to mock another's outcry until you know the burden they bear.

About The Editor

Clive Gilson was born in 1962 into a household steeped in sport and rhythm. His father was a senior amateur and lower-league professional footballer, while his mother, equally formidable, was an award-winning ballroom dancer. Their spirited household didn't just hum with ambition, it danced to it.

After earning a degree in History from Leeds University, Clive took an unexpected turn into the then-nascent world of information technology in the late 1980s. Yet, the call of story and stage never left him. Alongside a thriving tech career, he freelanced as a journalist and book reviewer, earning one small by-line in the national press, and also spent over a decade performing in village halls and professional theatres across the south of England.

A true inheritor of his family's sporting zeal, Clive later pivoted into live sports broadcasting. In the 1990s, he became a trusted rugby 'stato' for the BBC, ITV, EuroSport, and TVNZ, bringing insight and analysis to major tournaments including the Heineken Cup, Six Nations, World Sevens, and Rugby World Cups.

As a writer, Clive has made his mark across genres. His debut novel, *Songs of Bliss*, was published in 2017, followed by *A Solitude of Stars* in 2019. Since then, he has released three acclaimed short story collections, *The Mechanic's Curse*, *The Insomniac Booth*, and, in 2025, *Melodies in Black Ink*.

He is also an award-winning poet and the author of a biography detailing the life of a former professional footballer, namely his father. Since 2018, Clive has served as Managing Editor of the Firesides Tales Project, a global storytelling initiative that has published over 30 collections of folktales, fairy tales, myths, and legends from around the world.

Today, Clive continues to write fiction rich in folklore, memory, and quiet transformation, combining his deep love of narrative with a lifelong fascination with the human spirit.

For more about his work, visit clivegilson.com, where stories are always waiting to be found.

Pig Tails – Porcine Fairy Tales, Myths And Legends

ORIGINAL FICTION BY CLIVE GILSON

- *Songs of Bliss*
- *Out of the Walled Garden*
- *The Mechanic's Curse*
- *The Insomniac Booth*
- *A Solitude of Stars (Cry Havoc, part 1)*
- *A Symphony Of Sorrows (Cry Havoc, part 2)*
- *Melodies In Black Ink*
- *Acts Of Faith*

AS EDITOR – *FIRESIDE TALES – Western Europe*

- *Tales From the Land of Dragons* – Welsh Folk & Fairy Tales
- *Tales From the Land of The Brave* – Scottish Folk & Fairy Tales
- *Tales From the Land of Saints And Scholars* – Irish Folk & Fairy Tales
- *Tales From the Land of Hope And Glory* – English Folk & Fairy Tales
- *Tales from Gallia* – French Folk & Fairy Tales

AS EDITOR – *FIRESIDE TALES – Northern Europe*

- *Tales From Lands of Snow and Ice* – Scandinavian Folk & Fairy Tales
- *Tales From the Viking Isles* – Icelandic Folk & Fairy Tales
- *Tales From the Forest Lands* – Finnish Folk & Fairy Tales
- *Tales From the Old Norse* – Scandinavian Folk & Fairy Tales
- *Tales from Germania* – German Folk & Fairy Tales

AS EDITOR – *FIRESIDE TALES – Southern Europe*

- *Tales From the Land of Rabbits* – Spanish & Portuguese Folk & Fairy Tales
- *Tales Told by Bulls and Wolves* – Italian Folk & Fairy Tales
- *Tales of Fire and Bronze* – Greek Folk & Fairy Tales

AS EDITOR – *FIRESIDE TALES – Eastern Europe*

- *Tales From The Samodivi* – Balkan Folk & Fairy Tales
- *Tales From the Land of the Strigoi* – Romanian Folk & Fairy Tales

Pig Tails – Porcine Fairy Tales, Myths And Legends

- *Tales Told by the Wind Mother*– Hungarian Folk & Fairy Tales

AS EDITOR – *FIRESIDE TALES – North America*

- *Okaraxta* - Tales from The Great Plains
- *Tibik-Kìzis* – Tales from The Great Lakes & Canada
- *Jóhonaa'éí* –Tales from America's Southwest
- *Qugaaĝix̂* - First Nation Tales from Alaska & The Arctic
- *Karahkwa* - First Nation Tales from America's Eastern States
- *Pot-Likker* - Folklore, Fairy Tales, and Settler Stories from America

AS EDITOR – *FIRESIDE TALES – Africa*

- *Arokin Tales* – Folklore & Fairy Tales from West Africa
- *Hadithi Tales* – Folklore & Fairy Tales from East Africa
- *Inkathaso Tales* – Folklore & Fairy Tales from Southern Africa
- *Tarubadur Tales* – Folklore & Fairy Tales from North Africa
- *Elephant And Frog* – Folklore from Central Africa

AS EDITOR – *FIRESIDE TALES – Middle East*

- *Tales From The Meddahs* – Turkish Folk & Fairy Tales
- *Tales From The Hakawati* – Arabic Folk & Fairy Tales
- *Tales Told By Balebos & Gusan* – Jewish & Armenian Folk & Fairy Tales

AS EDITOR – *FIRESIDE TALES – Asia & The Far East*

- *Tales Told By The Kathaakaar* – Folk & Fairy Tales from India
- *Tales Of The Gùshì Yuan* – Chinese Folk & Fairy Tales

AS EDITOR – *FIRESIDE TALES – Animal Tales*

- *Dog Tails* – Folk & Fairy Tales featuring our canine chums
- *Cat Tails* – Folk & Fairy Tales featuring our feline friends
  Horse Tails – Folk & Fairy Tales featuring our equine pals
- *Pig Tails* – Folk & Fairy Tales featuring our porcine friends

Pig Tails – Porcine Fairy Tales, Myths And Legends

AS EDITOR – *FIRESIDE TALES – South & Central America*

- *Tales From The Caribbean* – Folk & Fairy Tales from Caribbean islands
- *Tales From Central America* – Central American Folk & Fairy Tales
- *Tales Told From South America* – South American Folk & Fairy Tales

Reviews

I have edited Clive Gilson's books for over a decade now – he's prolific and can turn his hand to many genres. poetry, short fiction, contemporary novels, folklore, and science fiction – and the common theme is that none of them ever fails to take my breath away. There's something in each story that is either memorably poignant, hauntingly unnerving, or sidesplittingly funny - *Lorna Howarth, The Write Factor*

Ragged A**** Ruffian reviewed on Amazon in the United Kingdom on 27 January 2021 - A truly heartwarming, interesting, story with a wonderful narrative. Unquestionably a splendid read

A Solitude of Stars: With deft turns of phrase and an imagination that would make Philip K. Dick jealous, Gilson foresees a dystopian future, the seeds of which are definitely being sown right now. The story is a chilling glimpse of what may come to pass, warmed by a thread of love that raises the narrative beyond despair. I found the stories disturbing and breath-taking in equal measure. The Apparat and Dirigiste tribes are ranging across our solar system seeking peace by waging war, raising the question; is humanity actually capable of peace? A riveting read. - *Rob Swan, The Write Factor*

Songs of Bliss gripped me from the start - I had to read right to the end. Loved the humour. Impressed by the surprising empathy that I felt for rather - on the face of it - unlikeable characters. Look forward to seeing it in print. - *Maighdean-Mhara, commenting on Authonomy*

I just wanted to thank you once more for your help acquiring this beautiful collection. It's found a new home at the top of my library. I've already stumbled onto some wonderful stories in a couple of the collections, and I can't wait to get more. Have a wonderful holiday and a great new year... - *Richer Daniel Laporte, California, December 2021*

Pig Tails – Porcine Fairy Tales, Myths And Legends

Melodies In Black Ink: A collection of darkly captivating short tales, each inspired by the melodies that move us, the lyrics that linger, and the stories hidden between the notes.

Gilson (editor of the international Fireside Stories series) offers a dark, poignant collection of genre-crossing stories, all inspired by songs, that explore the fragile intersections of love, loss, resilience, and the shadows we carry. Ranging from children with superpowers to accounts of blossoming love, abusive relationships, unexpected pregnancies, and the isolating rhythm of a machine-driven society, Gilson's stories capture raw textures of the human experience in a key suggested by their musical inspirations, which include lushly brooding tracks from Kate Bush, This Mortal Coil, Angel Olsen, The Cure, and Youssou N'Dour (the sublime "7 Seconds," a duet with Neneh Cherry.) Gilson has a gift for moment-to-moment storytelling that grips and then lingers, like Gorilla Glue stuck to one's fingertips, resisting even the harshest solvents of reason.

Life goes wrong in unpredictable yet resonant ways throughout these 26 compact tales, and Gilson's vivid portrayals of scenery and emotion make it easy to lose oneself in these narratives, drowning in a wave of feeling that refuses to let go. From the Scottish Highlands to space travel to the blood-soaked earth of Danish-Viking battlefields—told from the perspective of Ulfhednar and his sacred wolf, Ulric—these stories span wide imaginative terrain. Despite some big ideas and SF elements, characterization is compelling. "The Jakey and the Nae Chancer" introduces Elliot and Fiona, who have perfected the art of detachment, the latter of whom "was almost certain that her heart was too delicate to risk breaking again." One of the most heart-wrenching stories, "Be Well," is inspired by a devastating loss. It's a piece that does more than tug at the heart, it reaches in and seizes hold with unrelenting intensity.

Adding a unique dimension, each story concludes with a toast to the song and artist that inspired it, an invitation to experience these briskly potent stories on another sensory level, with a soundtrack tying words to melody, emotion to rhythm. Melodies in Black Ink is not light reading—but it is deeply moving, with haunting emotional rewards.

Searing, surprising stories of urgent feeling, inspired by beloved songs.

Pig Tails – Porcine Fairy Tales, Myths And Legends

The US Review of Books
Professional Reviews for the People

Melodies in Black Ink: This work is not just another set of tales linked together by a myriad of characters who sometimes appear in more than one narrative. In fact, this is much more than just another short story collection. It is also a reflective, musical journey. Accompanying each story is an explanation of the song that inspired the writing. Most impressive is the wide expanse of musical genres, artists, and songs included in this book. From Wardruna to Metric to Blue Oyster Cult to Dot Allison, the book's audience will experience a musical journey unlike any other. The incorporation of the notes discussing each inspirational song provides an informative background. It also provides historical context, along with the author's personal anecdotes, about each song.

What makes this book even more realistic is its honest, vulnerable, and sometimes gritty portrayal of the characters and their existences. One story in which all of these themes and characteristics culminate is "Going Underground." It is a story in which even the main character's name, Daniel Grimes, reflects the character's harsh, gritty environment and existence, as well as the difficult decisions Daniel must make. Daniel embodies rebellion against the status quo after having lived a life in which he originally "played by the rules. All it got him were ration credits and a little coin, enough to rent a bedsit and eat slop." "Going Underground" is a daring story with a dystopian tone. Deepening that dystopian tone is the fact that the author cleverly disguises the story's time period, and the tale can be read as either occurring in the past, the present, or the very near future.

Music lovers will appreciate this book because of the role music plays in each and every story. The stories, too, are a testament to not only the power of music but also of the necessity of interdisciplinary studies and the humanities. The stories are a novel type of ekphrastic writing in that, rather than responding to visual art, the stories are responses to music. The fluid, poetic writing in each story mirrors the magic and lyricism inherent in the songs the author utilizes. These stories are powerful, emotional, and moving. Most of all, they are beautifully and unquestionably human.

RECOMMENDED by the US Review

Book review by Nicole Yurcaba

www.ingramcontent.com/pod-product-compliance
Lightning Source LLC
Chambersburg PA
CBHW060543190726
48283CB00003B/850